DO YOU READ ME?

EIGHT SHORT STORIES BY JAN MARK

A group of zealous parish members are shocked to discover black magic in their well-tended graveyard . . .

Greg finds the perfect new wife for his father, but his father has other ideas . . .

Good-looking Daniel thinks nothing of not turning up for a date with Susie, that is until he is made to feel the force of woman's wrath . . .

This lively selection of Jan Mark's stories is guaranteed to intrigue and amuse you.

ABOUT THE AUTHOR

Jan Mark was born and brought up in Hertfordshire, though her family are from London. She began writing when she was very young, and won a *Daily Mirror* short story competition at the age of fifteen. She has won numerous awards since then for her writing and is regarded as one of the foremost writers for young people. Jan now lives in Oxford and has two children.

Do You Read Me ?

EIGHT STORIES BY

Jan Mark

HEINEMANN
NEW WINDMILLS

Heinemann Educational Publishers
Halley Court, Jordan Hill, Oxford OX2 8EJ
a division of Reed Educational & Professional Publishing Ltd
OXFORD   MELBOURNE   AUCKLAND
JOHANNESBURG   BLANTYRE   GABORONE
IBADAN   PORTSMOUTH (NH) USA   CHICAGO

First published in the New Windmill Series 1994

99 00 01 02 03 11 10 9 8 7 6 5 4

ISBN 0 435 12419 6

British Library Cataloguing in Publication Data
for this title is available from the British Library

Cover illustration by John Brennan

Typeset by CentraCet Limited, Cambridge
Printed and bound in England by Clays Ltd, St Ives plc

Contents

Too Old to Rock and Roll

"I think it might clear the air," Valerie said, "if you called a halt to the ongoing tit-for-tat situation."

"It's not tit-for-tat."

"All right, *quid pro quo*."

"What's that?"

"Up market tit-for-tat. But why not just lay off each other for a bit?"

"He started it," Greg said. "He shouldn't have called me a pimplie."

"And you shouldn't have called him a wrinklie."

"That's different. It's a sort of general term for anyone over – over – "

"Twenty-five? No need to be tactful," said Valerie, forty if a day. "Anyway, it makes no difference whether it's general or not, it still hurts."

"It's only a joke."

"If that's only a joke, so is pimplie. Added to which," Valerie said, "pimples go away, wrinkles don't."

"He's not all *that* wrinkled."

"Quite. And I suppose it was you who stuck that advert for the hair replacement therapy on the fridge."

"He's always going on about *my* hair."

"Call a truce," Valerie said. "It's very tedious listening to you two sparring all the time."

"We need a referee," Greg muttered.

"I know." Valerie's voice softened. "Well, anyway, I'll be round at eight. See you then, OK?"

1

He hung up and went into the kitchen. Valerie didn't miss a thing. It was only on Sunday that he had cut the advertisement from the Hogarth Hair Clinic out of *The Observer* and attached it to the side of the fridge with a magnet; the side that you saw first as you came in from the hall, along with cards for dental appointments and taxis, and the recipe in Mum's handwriting for avocado and chicken soup. It was half hidden under the bus timetable and Dad had missed it. Perhaps it was the only thing of Mum's left in the house, apart from the Christmas tree baubles. Greg slid it further under the timetable and looked at the clipping about the clinic. It advertised a new and revolutionary method of replacing lost growth – of hair, presumably, although it was too coy to come right out and say so – and showed a man's head, seen from above, on which growth had receded to a dim fringe around the ears, and next to it another picture of the same man, youthful and beaming and thatched like a yeti. Clients were advised to telephone the clinic for an appointment with the consultant trichologist before committing themselves to the course of treatment.

Greg could not really imagine his father slogging up to London regularly, not even for the initial appointment with the trichologist. In any case, his hair loss was nothing like so drastic as that threadbare dome in the picture. Standing up and walking about, Dad appeared to have a full head of hair, short but flourishing. It was only when seen from above, as Greg had discovered coming downstairs while Dad was on the phone in the hall, that the thinning patch on the crown was noticeable. Subsequently he had made one or two discreet surveys in passing, while Dad was watching television or sitting at the table, and realized that Dad had been already alerted to the problem, by his hairdresser, most likely. The latest

2

cut had the look of skilful topiary, every hair arranged to earn its place in the design. The advert on the fridge was intended more as a friendly hint than an insult, although Dad had not shown any signs of taking it either way. It had been there for three days and not a word spoken about it.

Still, Greg supposed, it was an optimistic omen, that hair cut, a sign that Dad was at last sitting up and taking notice. To be fair, he had been sitting up, as it were, for some time. The terrible paralysis that had struck him after Mum died had worn off after about four months, just in time for Christmas. It had been painful, Greg remembered, watching him constantly as he made himself get up, made himself read the paper, cut the hedge, cook a meal. What he had not seen, could only guess at, was Dad at work. In all that time he had driven off every morning, and driven himself through the day, doing whatever needed to be done, presenting a normal front to members of the public, presumably, and then coming home on autopilot and apparently operating on remote control for the rest of the evening. Somewhere inside that programmed android was Stephen Barber, reduced to a micro-chip that controlled the organism; the memory bank that directed the program. At work, Greg supposed, the routine had continued as usual; people came away with new glasses, contact lenses; no one was made blind. It hadn't functioned so well at home. The memory bank knew how to organize an optician, but not a single parent. Half of the working parts were missing.

That things were getting back to normal was due to Valerie. It was Valerie who had been there, entirely by chance, when the unhappy policeman had called to report the accident. Greg could no longer remember why she had been there; they knew her only slightly and it was Mum she had come to see, arriving at just around the time Greg and Dad had been starting to look at the clock and wonder why. She lived about thirty miles away, had a home of her own to go back to, cats to feed, plants to water, a theatre ticket in her purse for the following evening, but when the policeman had offered to drive them to the hospital Dad had turned to this virtual stranger and said, "Please stay", and so she had been there when they had returned, making, as Greg guessed later, a series of efficient phone calls back home; had remained until the life support system was switched off – that had been the worst daÿ – and withdrew tactfully for the funeral when the house had been filled with proprietorial Smiths and Barbers.

It was Valerie who had caused Christmas to happen. Greg himself had said nothing about it but Valerie's sensitive antennae had picked up the vibrations and for once she had abandoned tact.

"For Christ's sake, Steve!" he had heard her explode, down in the kitchen, "what about Greg?"

"He isn't interested in Christmas," Dad had said, in that heavy, dazed monotone. "How could he be? Frances *was* Christmas. She made it her own."

"I'll tell you what," Valerie said, brutally, "Frances must be spinning in her grave to see what a pig's ear you've made of surviving without her."

His father had gasped, audibly. "What an appalling thing to say."

"Why, because she *is* in her grave? Mourning her is one thing – but for how long? There's a lot to be said for an official period, after which you throw off your black crêpe and get back to normal. This is the rest of your life, Steve. It's the rest of Greg's life. Who do you think you are, Queen Victoria?"

"It's only four months."

"It's at *least* four months. If Christmas with Frances was so wonderful, isn't it worth trying to

4

keep it going? It was wonderful because she enjoyed it. It wasn't a chore to her, no nonsense about only doing it for the children. She enjoyed making it good for the three of you. How do you think she'd feel if you cared so little – ?"

"I care so much."

" – cared so little that you couldn't try to keep alive what she began."

"Christmas or Greg?"

"Good God, you made a joke," Valerie said.

Greg cornered her later while Dad went round to the off licence.

"Are you coming here for Christmas?"

Valerie looked at him sharply.

"Christmas? What made you think that?"

"It's the thirtieth of November," Greg said. "Isn't that time to be thinking of Christmas?"

"I usually visit my parents," Valerie said.

"They won't miss you just for once, will they?"

"I should think they might, actually."

"So would we," Greg said. He did not mean to be manipulative, but he knew that Valerie *must* be made to stay, because if this Christmas didn't happen, there might never be a Christmas again.

"Did you have a very special time?" Valerie asked, gently.

"We did it our own way," Greg said. "Mum's way. She hated Christmas beginning too soon, you know, cards in the shops in September and Santa's Grotto at Hallowe'en. We never did anything till December the first, with the Advent Calendar, then we used to send our cards, but we never put up decorations or dressed the tree till a week before Christmas. We usually did it on the evening after school broke up. We did it together."

"The three of you?"

"No, just me and her. Dad put the holly and stuff

5

up. The decorations are in a hat box – it was my great grandmother's – I used to get them out one at a time, and Mum would tell me where they came from. The first year they had their own home, and we were really hard up, Mum got a little tree – I thought it was huge because it was as tall as me – I was three, that's how little it was – she couldn't afford any decorations, and then she found this cornflakes box in the loft that had got left behind when the last people moved out, and there was all this tinsel in it, and some tree decorations. So she used them, and after that, every year, she'd buy some more, just two or three each time, but she still kept those first ones. Not the tinsel, you know how tinsel goes when it's old, but the baubles. They got broken, bit by bit, they were that very thin glass stuff, you know; but we've still got one of them. It looks a bit scruffy now, all the colour's come off, but we still use it. We always hang it up first of all. I've got the box in my room."

He had put it there when Dad started clearing everything out; clothes, jewellery, books, letters, and he had been wondering how and when to produce it. Now he knew.

"You *must* come," he said to Valerie.

"If I'm asked."

"I'm asking."

"We'll have to work on it," Valerie said.

"Won't one of your neighbours feed the cats?"

"I wasn't thinking of the cats." Valerie, sitting at the kitchen table competently slicing onions for spaghetti bolognese, had paused and looked straight at him.

"It'll be hard work, Greg. We almost left it too late."

"For Christmas."

"For Steve. Perhaps we've been soft-pedalling for too long. I don't know if you heard us just now – yes,

6

you did, of course you did — well, I said something really unkind, something I wouldn't have dreamed of saying normally, and he actually snapped at me; answered back. That's the first time I've seen any signs of animation since Frances died.

"I've been admiring you, Greg, for the way you've coped — coped with Steve, as much as anything. And I suddenly thought, Dammit, I like this man. I don't want to feel sorry for him, I want to admire him, too, so I said . . . what I did say, and I think it worked. This is a shocking thing to suggest to a respectable teenager, but Greg, I think you might try being a little ruder, now and again. Be a bit selfish."

"Cruel to be kind?"

"Yes — but not too cruel."

Had he been too cruel? It was past Easter now, the tree decorations long back in their box, the presents tarnished with familiarity, the tree itself still moulting brown spines at the end of the garden.

He had waited until Christmas Eve before taking Valerie's advice, keenly observing the situation, calculating the optimum moment to slip his stiletto between the armour plating, then standing back, breathless, to discover whether he had lanced a boil or punctured a vital organ.

In the afternoon when Dad came home from a solitary tour of the supermarket and before Valerie arrived from Ipswich, he had dug out the hat box from where he had buried it at the bottom of the wardrobe, and clattered *cheerfully* downstairs with the box under his arm. His father looked out of the kitchen doorway, haggard, sunken-eyed, stooped.

"What have you got there?"

Greg raised the box like a trophy.

"The tree decorations."

Dad had advanced from the doorway with something like rage in his eyes.

"Where did you find them?"

"Didn't find them," Greg said pertly, over his shoulder, and went into the living room. "I hid them in the wardrobe. Didn't want you throwing *them* out."

Dad followed him into the undecorated, unheated room. "Why have you brought them down?"

"To put on the tree."

"What tree? We aren't having a tree. How could you – "

"*I* want a tree," Greg said, baldly. "Mum wouldn't have wanted to spoil my Christmas." That was when he had paused, waiting to see what effect his effrontery would have. His father stood looking round slowly, seeming to awake to something he had not seen before, at Greg, and away again, then at his watch.

"It's too late to get a tree now," he said, hopelessly.

"Valerie's bringing it with her," Greg said, "and some holly. Shall I light the fire?"

After that it had been easier; the occasional back-chat, a light-hearted insult, a show of the ill temper he had been carefully, fearfully, suppressing for so long, until they were sniping regularly, amicably, as they had always done. And Valerie, after that Christmas visit, came more often, stayed longer, until the spare room became known as Valerie's room. No one else wanted to use it.

But had he gone too far with the Hogarth Hair Clinic advertisement? Repeated gibes about flares and ageing trendies had finally provoked Dad into going out and buying some new clothes to replace the disintegrating favourites that Mum had chosen for him, but anyone, at any age, needed new clothes from time to time. Suggesting that somebody needed new hair was near unforgiveable.

Greg lifted the magnet and slid out the offending square of newsprint, screwed it into a ball and chucked it into the swing bin. He moved the magnet round to the door of the fridge, which was the place for messages, slipped a sheet of paper under it and wrote in violent and unmissable green felt tip:

GONE TO BAND PRACTICE. VAL RANG.
WILL BE HERE AT EIGHT.

Then he put the casserole in the oven, turned on the gas, mark 2, and went to check that the table was properly laid in the dining room. It was his pleasure now to know that when Valerie arrived it would be to a table exquisitely prepared, white napkins, gleaming glassware, flowers and candles, and to Dad, who would have had an hour or so to prepare himself exquisitely instead of batting distractedly round the kitchen, dropping grease and bean sprouts, before dropping a charred pie dish on the table and ripping off sheets of kitchen roll because the napkins hadn't been washed from last time. When Greg came home at nine they would be sitting relaxed in the front room, pleasantly boozed up and ready to eat the meal that awaited only Greg's last loving attentions before appearing on the table along with hot rolls, butter pats, green salad and a nice red wine, properly *chambré*. At the front door he paused to switch on the porch light in readiness, and looked back to make sure that nothing was out of place. He hated to acknowledge it – and Dad never would, but even Mum had never been this well organized.

The band practices took place at Mark's house because Mark's house was detached and both his parents worked late shifts, but principally because Mark was the drummer and the least mobile. Greg

9

was the roadie, which meant, since none of them was old enough to drive, that when they played a gig he was responsible for loading all the equipment and the drums on to Mark's father's trailer and hauling it through the streets to the Co-op Hall or the room over the Prince of Wales. Toby, the lead guitarist, had lettered a banner with the band's name, MEANS TEST, long enough to tack round three sides of the trailer.

The band was high minded and accepted only politically correct engagements: Rock Against Racism, Rock Against the Poll Tax and Rock on behalf of anyone who happened to be on strike. Toby was a tireless monitor of Trade Union discontent and made forecasts, sometimes months in advance, of who was likely to come out next. Toby's father was a Conservative councillor, but permissibly wet. Greg occasionally suspected that he himself had been admitted to Means Test solely on the grounds that his old man had been seen on the streets canvassing for Labour at the last election. As roadie he had little to do on practice nights unless Morris, the bass guitarist, had had an asthma attack, but he had joined them in the New Year as much to establish a reason for going out as a need to make music.

"Music?" Dad said, morosely, "or Rock and Roll?"

"Rock, not Roll," Greg had said, daring him to imply that wanting to play in a rock band so soon – five months, by then – was unfeeling, unseemly, unfilial. But Dad had said nothing about that, had said only, "Had a good time?" when he returned and had thereafter refrained from comment when he started playing records again, up in the bedroom.

When the practice ended, just before nine, Mark produced cans of lager from the fridge, Morris said he had enough blow for one roll-up and Means Test settled in for a dissolute evening. Greg made his excuses and left.

"Want to get back and catch them at it?" Toby inquired as he went out, but no, that was not what he wanted at all. He wanted to be at home, opening the back door to an odour of hot, cooked food, to hear contented voices from the living room, to take a beer and go in and join them for half an hour before they all sat down to his casserole and he could enjoy Valerie's compliments about his cooking and his table laying. He said nothing of this, however. Wanting to be cosy at home was not part of the Rock ethos.

"Got an assignment to finish," he said, and departed in a chorus of friendly groans.

The light was on in the living room when he approached the house. Dad was standing in there alone, his back to the window, but Valerie's car was in the drive; she must have left the room for something. As Greg opened the gate he saw her through the dappled glass of the front door, advancing down the lighted hall and turning right into the living room. And as she did, his father left the window and moved forward, his arms held wide. Greg proceeded to the back door very slowly. The last thing he wanted to do was catch them at it and spoil everything.

He could hardly take the credit for having made it happen, but he had done all he could to help things along, making sure that Valerie knew she was welcomed by at least one member of the household, even in the worst days when Dad had wanted to see no one; making sure that Dad knew how much he liked Valerie. He was in no hurry. He was not keen for either of them to think that he wanted to replace Mum, that he had forgotten her already, that he did not miss her constantly to the extent that when he saw the house in his mind's eye she was always in it.

11

He still expected to see her in the garden, he still did see her out shopping, in cars, on a bus, her very self, until the features inevitably dissolved into someone else, someone who did not resemble her at all. But he was sure that Valerie never supposed for one moment that he had forgotten. And Dad had never shown signs of understanding that he felt anything at all.

When he went into the front room they were sitting down again, either side of the unlit fire. On the hearth was a big earthenware jug that Mum had found in an Oxfam shop, filled with tulips, red, pink, orange, yellow; all the colours of flame, blazing coolly.

"Valerie brought them," Dad said, and Greg saw that he was smiling, a real, effortless smile, not the miserable rictus he had forced in company as though taught how to do it by a physiotherapist. Greg had seen Valerie's garden, compact and brilliant inside its trellised walls, like a box of flowers behind her ground floor flat. The three cats had lain in the spring sunshine on a lawn the size and texture of a carpet. Even in March the French doors had stood open to the sheltered air. Would Valerie want to leave all that?

He looked at her, smiling back at Dad. Was she *expecting* some reward for her kindness, for her devotion to two near strangers, the husband and son of a friend, or had she considered it a moral duty, or had she just seen that it needed doing and done it, and was now taking pleasure purely in her success? Then he looked again at Dad; something was different, something had changed, not just the smile and the haircut, there was something else that he had seen without really noticing, when he saw Dad in the window. It was his clothes, a new black sweater over a striped shirt, and *jeans*. His father was wearing jeans.

"I thought it was time I had some new gear," Dad

said, looking almost sheepish, but mostly pleased with himself – for the effort rather than the effect, Greg thought. "I can't go on shaming you in public."

Wow! Sarcasm. Was it just possible that everything was going back to normal, that the man sitting there by the fireside was slowly being transformed back into Stephen Barber, the humorous, handsome man he had grown up with, the man who had married Mum – was he coming home again?

"Do you want a drink?" Valerie asked him, "or are you ready for us to eat? Your casserole smells wonderful." She said nothing about Dad's new turn-out, but there was no need to say anything. Each knew how pleased and relieved the other was.

At dinner Dad was more than courteous, courtly, almost, as if trying to make a good impression, seeing Valerie for the first time, or for the first time as a woman, at any rate.

Toby had been very wide of the mark in his assumption that Dad and Valerie were having it off. This was the first time that Greg had seen him deliberately aiming to please her, to attract her attention. Once he would not have had to try. Women had been charmed by him simply because he was there. Greg recalled dropping in at the optician's on the way home from school, because it had looked empty of customers and he fancied a chat. The two lady assistants had seemed resentful and embarrassed, Dad awkward, not quite himself.

Mum had laughed when he told her. "Don't for God's sake do that again. They both flirt like mad with him and they're insanely jealous of each other."

"What about you?" he'd asked, indignantly.

"Me? They probably think I don't understand him and ruined his life. I expect they secretly pray that I'll fall under a bus."

He'd forgotten that crack. It hadn't been a bus, in

the event. Her car had collided with a blameless milk float, an accident seemingly so slight that it was difficult to take it seriously, hard to believe that someone had died in it. He sometimes wondered what the two jealous women in the shop had thought. He remembered their wreath: chrysanthemums. What *had* they thought? Had they privately begun to hope?

They were both young and quite pretty; Yvonne and Denise, and then there was Mary Dane who came in on Wednesday afternoons, and, of course, Susannah, Mrs Shannon, who was the other optician. What *had* they all thought, wondered, hoped? What would they think if they could see Valerie, who was not very young or very pretty – but right, absolutely right.

"I'll wash up," he said.

"Oh no, that's not fair," Valerie protested. "You cooked it all."

"I've started so I'll finish," he said. "You go and sit in the other room."

"We'll wash up together," Dad said, managing to make it sound like a long-promised treat, so Greg went upstairs, left his door ajar, and listened to them in the kitchen, laughing, talking, late into the night, and then silence.

Next morning he refused to satisfy his curiosity about which room Valerie had slept in, and went out before either of them was up. He helped out at a bakery on Saturday mornings, from seven o'clock, so there was no question of delivering early morning tea and an awkward juggling of trays while he listened at keyholes.

So, no, he hadn't been too cruel and Valerie had been right. Between them they had jolted Dad back to life, like electrodes applied to a heart that had stopped beating.

During the following week Dad bought some more clothes for both of them. Greg prudently asked for the money and did his own shopping, since Means Test had agreed that they would play in collarless shirts, black trousers and high laced boots. Dad would never have demurred at any of this but he would not have thought of it unprompted although, Greg had to admit, the clothes that he was buying for himself were a lot more fashionable than the things he had worn when Mum was alive. He even stopped wearing a suit to work and went out in a jacket that Greg could imagine himself considering in a year or two. At the weekend, when Valerie came over, they went out on Saturday and Sunday.

"Do you want to come?" Dad said, with what Greg hopefully recognized as a distinct lack of enthusiasm.

"Not with exams coming up," Greg said virtuously, and from his bedroom window watched them get into the car and drive away. The thinning patch in Dad's hair hardly showed with that new cut, in fact he had been back to the hairdresser since and had some more topiary. When he closed the passenger door for Valerie he *ran* round to the driver's side, slim and agile in his jeans and tailored shirt. Greg normally drew the line at tailored shirts but on Dad they looked good and showed how flat his stomach was. Greg, satisfied, settled down to his revision.

On Wednesday Dad came home earlier than usual.

"Do you mind fending for yourself tonight?" he asked. Greg heard the bath running.

"Going out?"

"A party."

"A *party*?" Dad at a party? "Where?"

"Yvonne's getting engaged. You know, Yvonne at the shop."

Greg had imagined that Yvonne might be getting big ideas, the way Dad was turning out. He had not thought of her having a private life away from the shop, with a family, boy friends.

"Where does she live?"

"Oh, out past the ring road. I've got the address somewhere. I don't suppose I'll be very late but don't wait up."

"Won't it be a bit of a rave-up?" Greg asked, dubiously. "I mean, she's only about twenty-something, isn't she?"

"Twenty-six."

"They'll all be bopping. You won't like the music."

Dad looked irritated. "How do you know I won't like the music?"

"You don't like mine," Greg said.

"Yvonne's friends are likely to be a good bit older than you."

"And a good bit younger than *you*," Greg muttered.

"I heard that. Why do you suppose Yvonne invited me?"

"Out of politeness?" Greg suggested. "You're her boss. I don't expect she thought you'd say yes. Is Valerie going?"

"Valerie? Of course not."

"She might like to go to a party."

"Oh, for heaven's sake, she's probably got better things to do. I can't haul her over here for that."

He bounded upstairs again; bounded. Greg tried to recall if Dad had ever been to a party with Mum; they'd gone out to dinner parties often enough, and evenings spent informally with friends, but never a party, with dancing, with people twenty years younger. It was unhealthy, degrading; no wonder he didn't want Valerie to see him making a fool of himself.

He went out half an hour later, in new shoes. Greg regretted throwing away the advertisement for the Hogarth Hair Clinic. It ought to be right there on the fridge, where he would see it when he came in. He wasted ten minutes searching through the Sunday paper for an ad he remembered seeing about face lifts. It was after midnight when Dad came home.

Valerie arrived as usual on Friday evening. Greg gave Means Test a miss after ringing Morris to make sure that he was in good health, and produced a lavish salad with chilled cucumber soup. When he heard her car pull up on the gravel of the drive he went into the kitchen to prepare the drinks – G and T for Valerie, beer for himself and Scotch on the rocks for Dad – to give Dad a chance to go to the door and enjoy his greeting in private. He opened bottles, cans, poured liquid, dropped in ice cubes, but the door did not open. Instead he heard the bell ring and, when no one responded, went to answer it himself. Once upon a time he had always done this, virtually lying in wait for his first sight of the car coming up the road, but for the last few weeks it had been Dad who lay in wait. Why didn't the silly sod take his chance now?

Valerie was on the doorstep, overnight bag in one hand, off-licence carrier in the other.

"Hullo, Greg, take the bottles, will you? There's something else in there for you."

"Thanks – let's have your case." He ushered her in. "I don't know where Dad's got to – he was here just now. Go into the front room, I'm just getting your drink."

"What a good host you are," Valerie said, surrendering both bags. "Everyone should have someone like you to come home to."

The telephone gave a sharp ping. They waited for it to begin ringing.

"Somebody changed their minds?" Valerie said.

17

"No, Dad must have put the extension down upstairs."

He went back to the kitchen. The phone was by the bed for emergencies – Mum had been a midwife – but Dad usually made his calls in the hall. Greg emptied the carrier bag; Muscadet in the fridge, they could have that later. Fitou, that would go nicely with his *boeuf bourguignon* tomorrow; and for him? There was something long and slim, wrapped in tissue, a proper cook's knife. Only last week he'd been bitching about the state of the kitchen equipment. He tested the blade; perfect; lethal; he could hardly wait to get at Saturday's beef.

Dad came downstairs at last and went into the front room. Greg decelerated his preparations to give them a decent interval before carrying in the tray. Dad and Valerie were in the right places, and seemed to have been there for some time.

"I was just saying, I shan't be here tomorrow," Dad was saying.

"Not at all?"

"Oh, I'll be back in the evening, but I'll have to go into the shop."

"You were in last week . . . weren't you?" Dad took turns with Susannah Shannon to cover Saturdays.

"Yes, but she just rang, she can't make it this week. We'll square it another time. Still, you can entertain each other, can't you?"

"Rather short notice, isn't it?" Greg said, disapprovingly. It was not until later, when he was spooning cream into the cucumber soup, that it occurred to him that no one had rung up. Dad had made the call.

Greg did the washing on Saturday mornings as Mum had always done. Valerie volunteered to prepare a light lunch to keep them going until the *boeuf bourguignon* that evening. Greg, in the hall, looked back at the comfortable sight of her figure bent over

18

the working surface, grating cheese, and nipped upstairs to his father's room; closed the door and rang the optician's.

"May I speak to Mr Barber, please?"

"I'm afraid he's not in today." Denise had not recognized his voice. "Would you like to speak to Mrs Shannon or shall I take a message?"

"No, thank you," Greg said. "It's personal."

That would set them wondering, but it was personal. It was. It was.

"See you next week," Valerie said, on the doorstep, Sunday evening. She was speaking to Greg but it was Dad who answered.

"I'm not sure. Can I ring you?"

"Well — yes, of course;" Valerie sounded faintly surprised. Greg was more than faintly surprised and, at the same time, not surprised at all.

"What's happening next week, then?" he said, as the tail lights disappeared at the end of the road. He waved, one last salute as always, but Dad was already back indoors.

"I said, what's happening next week?" He advanced down the hall. "Where will we be?"

"Here . . . I don't know." Dad was looking the other way, not at anything, just the other way.

"*I'll* be here."

"Look, it's not a regular thing, is it?"

"What isn't?"

"Valerie coming here."

"Yes it is."

"Well, I might be doing something else next weekend."

"*What?*"

"What the hell's it got to do with you?"

"I want to see Valerie next weekend." Greg felt his lip trembling.

19

"Why don't you go there?"

"She hasn't asked me."

"I'll ask *her*," Dad said, brightly, turning. "She must be sick of trekking over here every week."

"No she's not."

"How do you know? Look, it's not – it's – it's unfair to involve someone else too much with our problems."

"Problems? Involve?"

"Valerie's a friend, she's a good friend, she's done so much for us," Dad was gabbling now, "but we can't expect her to go on . . . to go on . . ."

"To go on with what?"

"To go on. I mean, she's only a friend."

"Only a friend?" Greg saw the lights come on. "But I thought you – and her . . ."

"No."

"What did you expect?" Toby asked, cleaning his fingernails with a plectrum. "He's free, he's got over your mum, he wants to start again."

"What about Valerie?"

"Oh, come *on*," Toby sighed; "she's too old for him."

"They're the same age. I asked her."

"There you are, I've seen her, remember. She looks her age, he doesn't. And he doesn't want to be seen with someone like that. People will think he can't do any better for himself. Poor old Steve, can't pull the birds any more."

The bird that Dad had pulled was twenty-four and looked eighteen.

"God, aren't you clever. I wish I could cook," she said, when Greg served a ratatouille on Friday evening.

"Can't you?" he said, chillingly.

Dad looked at her damply and fondled her shoulder.

"I should learn, if I were you," Greg advised her. "I shan't always be here." And neither will you, he added, silently.

Just Passing Through

We found Mr Mortimore through a card in the window of the post office. It was a lucky break, Mum said, because left to himself, Mr Mortimore would never have found us (although she was wrong about that). No one can find Rutland Street. Even if you ask directions from people who have lived round here all their lives, they have to stop and think hard; then they make excuses about the one-way system, especially if you are in a car, but even now I often miss the turn when I come home by bike in the dark. Rutland Street is a street only in the middle; at either end it is an alley. You can just get a car through from Hurst Street, but in St Mary's Road it's hardly more than a gap between two houses.

Still, as far as it goes, which isn't far, it's a proper street, only scaled down, little terraced houses either side, two strips of pavement and a bit of roadway, not two metres wide. The council have painted double yellow lines down both sides.

"Rutland Street?" said Mr Mortimore, when Mum rang him up. "Hang on, don't tell me . . . off Iffley Road – no, tell a lie, Catherine Street!"

"Hurst Street."

"That's right," said Mr Mortimore, generously. "Of course, I ought to know, considering . . ."

"Considering what?" Eric asked, when Mum told us about the conversation.

"He didn't say."

"Probably born here," Dad said. "Went out one day and never found his way back."

"Well, is he going to come?" I said.

"Of course he's going to come," said Mum. "Why else would he advertise?"

Mr Mortimore's postcard said that he specialized in all kinds of household repairs and maintenance, also gardening. The last bit wasn't important. Our back garden is seven metres long and the front garden only runs to centimetres, but we wished we'd known about Mr Mortimore when we first moved in. Before we bought the house it had been rented to people who didn't care that it sagged and leaked and had no damp course. Mum and Dad did wonders by their standards, but Dad still reads everything in feet and inches, even on a metric rule, which is why the house is slowly turning into a polyhedron, and Mum, being an archaeologist, knows more about Neolithic undertakers than she does about Victorian builders. With a second wet winter threatening, they called Rotman in.

He was really Mr Ennals from South Midlands Proofing Systems, but he rammed up Rutland Street in a red VW, and leaped out in scarlet overalls, superhero style, so ever after he was known as Rotman. As it turned out, we didn't have rot, wet or dry, woodworm, deathwatch beetle or dutch elm disease. What we had was rising damp. Rotman left us an estimate and it was while Mum and Dad were arguing over the estimate and some bank statements, that I noticed Mr Mortimore's advert.

"He's got to be cheaper than Rotman," Mum said, wanly, for by now the mortgage was biting deep and the money was running out. When he arrived he looked cheaper than Rotman. He came up Rutland Street next Saturday morning on a bicycle, with a little wooden trailer bumping behind it. We watched him padlock the bike to our front railings, and the trailer to next door's.

"Dr Clegg?" he asked, when Dad answered the door.

"No, that's Dr Clegg," Dad said, pointing to Mum.

"You at the health centre?" Mr Mortimore asked, stepping in.

"Not that sort of doctor," Mum said.

"Thought I didn't know the name. Been here long?" All the time he was peering at the plaster and knocking his knuckles against the woodwork.

"A year."

Mr Mortimore bounced on the rogue floorboard at the foot of the stairs. "Sprung," he said. "Had the floor up?"

"I think we have that pleasure to come," Dad said. Rotman had raised a plank or two and sucked his teeth, but he'd missed that one.

"Done any plastering lately?" He looked at the awkward bit above the door lintel. "I don't reckon you've got a single right angle in the whole place."

Eric and I stood on the stairs and watched Mr Mortimore progress through the house. It was like a keen gardener passing a weedy flower bed, he couldn't keep his hands off. At last Mum got him out to the back lobby and our dodgy damp patch.

"When we moved in," Dad said, "the agent thought it might be the plumbing."

"Could be," Mr Mortimore said, thumbing it. Eggshell emulsion came off on his hand.

"No," said Mum. "When it rains, the tidemark rises."

"Rises, you say?"

"Rises. It is rising damp, isn't it?"

Mr Mortimore was looking thoughtful. "It doesn't, as you might say, have a tendency to move sideways? It doesn't spread?"

"Well, it does spread," Mum said. "It would, wouldn't it?"

"And it always goes back again?"

"When the rain stops, yes."

"And does it, perhaps, rise a little higher each time?"

"Well, marginally."

"And it doesn't have any particular preference as to which way it goes?"

"It goes up!" Mum said. "It rises. Rising damp."

There was a long pause, then:

"That's all right then," Mr Mortimore said.

Dad noticed us hovering. "Didn't you say something about shopping?" he said, heavily. "Something about paying the paper bill . . .?" I could see his point. It is a very small house and five of us squeezed into the back lobby gave you some idea of what the Black Hole of Calcutta must REALLY have been like. We went off and did all the things we usually do on a Saturday morning before the weekend properly gets going, but when we came back Mr Mortimore was still there. Dad had gone out. Mum and Mr Mortimore were having coffee in the kitchen.

"The fact is," Mr Mortimore was saying, "I've done some work here before, years ago."

"In this house?" Mum said.

"That's what I can't be sure about," Mr Mortimore said. "I hope not. I hope it wasn't this one."

"Well, if it was so long ago . . ."

"Forty-one years. Just after my fourteenth birthday."

"The houses here are so alike – "

"Identical, as it happens," Mr Mortimore said. "Seven each side, all the same."

"Not any more," Mum said. Most of the streets in East Oxford are terraced, but they didn't get like that all at once. If you look you can see that to start with

25

there were perhaps a couple of farm cottages, then someone built on half-a-dozen others, then there'd be two big semis, then another row, and so on, all similar but not identical. Rutland Street isn't like that. The two terraces were built exactly the same, as Mr Mortimore said, three up, two down and a kitchen stuck out at the back. But people are modernizing them. All the old sash windows are going and in some of the houses the third bedroom, over the kitchen, had become a bathroom. The Ahmeds, next door, have done that, and several people have put an extra room in the loft. Our bathroom is built on downstairs, beyond the kitchen, and the rising damp was where the new bit meets the old.

"When I was last here," Mr Mortimore said, "there wasn't a ha'p'orth of difference between any of them, which is why I can't remember which one we were in before. All I know, it was an end one, on the left. Trouble is, I'm not sure WHICH end."

"Rising damp – "

" – the same. To start with, that is," he added.

"It wasn't rising damp?"

"More like sidling damp," Mr Mortimore said, after a moment, "which is why I expressed an interest, if you'll forgive me, in which way YOURS is going."

"Up," Mum said, firmly. "Really, Mr Mortimore, it IS rising."

"So did the other, at the beginning," he said. "Started off as a little patch, no bigger than a man's hand, just above the skirting board. We were actually called in, me and my dad, to look at the wiring, and the lady, Mrs Minton, her name was, says to my dad, afterwards, 'Mr Mortimore, I'd be glad if you'd take a look at this here' – and she leads us out to this very spot – if this IS the same house," he added, rather hurriedly, I thought. "Of course, there was no bathroom, then, it was an outside wall; and there's this damp patch, just coming up."

" 'Been there long?' says my dad.

" 'It seems to have come overnight,' she says.

" 'Been a very wet autumn,' says my dad. 'Leave it be a bit and see if it goes away again.'

"Well, to cut a long story short," Mr Mortimore went on, "it didn't. We went back a few days later and Mrs Minton says, 'No, it hasn't gone yet.' And when we looked, it certainly hadn't. Three feet up the wall it was, now, long and thin, not so much a hand more like someone was putting their arm up for something, like at school. Still, there was Christmas coming and it didn't seem very urgent; so we left it. It wasn't something to keep you awake at nights. WASN'T. . ."

Mum kept looking out through the kitchen door to where OUR damp patch was. I could just see it from where I was standing. It seemed to have risen a bit higher since I last saw it, about an hour before, but I might have been imagining that.

"Well, just before New Year," Mr Mortimore was saying, "there comes this knocking on our door and there's Mrs Minton's youngest on the step, very agitated. – Will we come and look at Mother's trouble? It was growing.

"Off we went together, me and Dad. Mother's trouble had certainly grown. Right up the wall it was, and BULGING a bit.

" 'That's come on fast,' says Dad, which it had, being now about as big as him and reaching to his head height. It was much the same shape, too, sort of dwindling away towards the foot – not that I mean anything in particular by that word, Doctor – just where it came up out of the skirting board. 'I have never before seen rising damp like that,' says my Dad – and," Mr Mortimore proclaimed, "I might add that

27

I have never seen anything like it since." He looked over his shoulder towards the kitchen door.

"Well, it was late in the afternoon, dark setting in, mortally cold. They were wicked winters that come on after the war," Mr Mortimore said. He rang our radiator with his knuckles. "No central heating in those days. 'We'll be back tomorrow,' Dad says. 'Dig about a bit.'"

"Next morning we wrapped up warm. Dad's got his toolkit, I'm carrying the pickaxe, and off we go. It was raw; not freezing, raw. Made your skin feel like meat just out of the fridge. You could see your breath, but it looked like fog, not mist. We came into Rutland Street and our footsteps went before us, solemnly. You've noticed that echo, I daresay. It gave me a cold grue this morning when I heard my trailer bumping up the street behind me, and that old echo up ahead. Rang like cracked bells, our boots did, as we came down the alley."

"Which end did you come in from?" Eric said, quickly. We were beginning to think that this might be important.

"That's what I can't recall."

"Must have been from Hurst Street," I said. "You don't get much of an echo coming the other way."

"Ah, but you did then," Mr Mortimore said. "In those days there was only an alley through from Hurst Street, too. That was before they widened it, when Heaton's bakery came down. Anyway, as we arrived, out comes young Minton, waving his arms.

"'You're too late!' he yells. 'You're too late! It's getting away!'

"'What do you mean, you young lunatic?' says my dad – but we saw soon enough what he meant. The whole family was there, seven of them without their father; he went in '43 – tail gunner. You wouldn't think you could fit so many into a place this size.

28

Anyway, there they all were, where we are now – if this IS the same house," he interrupted himself nervously, "and there in front of them was the damp patch and, damn me, it HAD got away. During the night it had moved up."

"Risen higher, you mean?" Mum said, and I noticed we were all craning our necks to see round the corner into the lobby.

"Oh yes," Mr Mortimore said, "it had risen higher, but it hadn't got any bigger. It was a good twelve inches clear of the skirting board and where it had been before, the wall was utterly dried out, as if it had never been. Moreover," said Mr Mortimore impressively, "it wasn't going up, any more. It had tilted a bit; heading for the corner of the ceiling, it seemed to me.

"'This is very interesting,' says my dad, which of course it was. 'Perhaps if you could clear some space?' he says, not addressing anyone in particular, you understand, and after a bit all the Mintons started to move away. While they were milling about I went over to the wall, very casual, and put my hand on the damp patch. It was soft," Mr Mortimore said, "like touching cold soft flesh. I wouldn't have been surprised if it had shrunk away from my hot touch like a slug, not that I wasn't surprised enough anyway. And thinking of slugs," he went on, "made me look at that great damp patch and that's when I saw that it was moving."

"Rising," Mum said. There was something almost pathetic about the way she kept saying "rising", as if it was the only safe thing TO say.

"You saw it move?" I said. I was thinking of slugs, too; the way they surge inside themselves as they move forward.

"I didn't see movement as such," Mr Mortimore said, "no more as you actually see a flower open, or a cloud change shape. But when I looked down I saw that the bottom of the damp had moved a couple of inches, and while I was looking at that, something else was going on up above, 'cause when I looked up again the patch had changed shape – and it was a lot closer to the corner, sort of stretching out towards it."

"Like an amoeba?" Eric said.

"Like an arm," said Mr Mortimore. "Dad had stepped outside to fetch the tools that he'd dumped in the hall. He came back just then and stood looking over my shoulder, then he said, 'That there is on the move.' It was a very dramatical moment," said Mr Mortimore.

It was pretty dramatical for us, and it was too much for Eric. He slipped out of the door and went to have a close look at OUR damp stain.

"What's it doing?" Mum asked.

"Not a lot," Eric said, and managed to sound relieved and disappointed all at once.

"You have to WATCH it," Mr Mortimore said. "That is, if yours is going the same way as that other, you'd have to stand and observe it. Like we did," he said. "Minute by minute, inch by inch – I won't weary you with the details, but the whole morning we stood turns, watching that creeping thing. Not that we ever saw it creep. You looked up, and there it was, groped forward, and while you was looking at that, it hauled itself up from below. You looked down, and forwards it went at the top. What we wanted to know," Mr Mortimore said, "was what it would do when it got to the ceiling."

His cup was empty. Mum poured him another.

"What did it do?" Eric said.

"As far as we could see, at first," said Mr Mortimore, "nothing. When it reached the top of the wall it started to get smaller. It didn't spread across the ceiling, it just bulged a bit, like it was constricted, at an angle, and gradually vanished away. Then my dad said, 'It's my belief it's gone upstairs. With your permission, we'll take a look,' he says to Mrs Minton, so up we go, her and him and I and several little Mintons (not that you could tell them apart) and when we went into the back bedroom, there it was, EMERGING, down along the skirting board, making its way in a north-easterly direction. Not this bedroom up above us," he said, pointing to the ceiling, "it had gone kitty-corner, through the joist, very direct.

"My dad says to me, 'Cut back down and see what's happening below.' But of course, the whole herd comes down with me, and when I got out here – or there," he amended, "it was disappearing. All that was left was a little wet soft blob, and the rest of the wall was as dry as old bones, flat as an ironing board. And my dad looked up to where the thing had gone, and he said, 'In my opinion, Mrs Minton, it won't be troubling you much longer.' And he was right. When we came back after dinner, lunch you probably call it, there was barely a yard between the head of that thing and the party wall.

"'Tell me,' says my dad, to Mrs Minton, 'are you by way of being friends with the people next door?'

"'We exchange a civil word of a morning,' says Mrs Minton.

"'Next civil word you exchange,' says my dad, 'you might inquire if they're having any problems with their plaster. Your damp patch is about to become their damp patch. Now it's clear of the ground it's travelling at will and gathering speed. I calculate it should be through by midnight.' Well," Mr Mortimore said, "as we went home through the chilly streets, my dad outlines his plan.

"'Tomorrow morning,' he says, 'you stroll on down to Mrs M, and ask her how things are, round about ten o'clock. That should have given her time to exchange her civil word. I think we'll find her problem has passed on.' So, next morning out I went –

New Year's Eve, you'll recall – and down along to Rutland Street, but before I got to Mrs Minton, I'm waylaid by a party who leaps out at me.

"'Aren't you Mortimore's boy?' she says. I had to agree. 'You tell him to step along later and look at my wall.'

"Hullo, I thought, things are moving, because, Dr Clegg, this person was not Mrs Minton's next-door neighbour, she was next-but-one.

"'Do you want me to take a look?' I said, halfway to her door already. Wild horses would not have kept me out. 'I can report back to dad in detail,' I said. So she looked a bit sniffy, but up she went, straight upstairs. 'Here,' she says, behind me, 'how do you know where to look?'

"'Instinct, Ma'am,' I said, and opened the door of the back bedroom. And I was right. It was just on its way along from next door, having passed straight through during the small hours, I suppose, that damp unwholesome swollen thing, all sagging and bulging along the skirting board. And a very noisome odour with it, now.

"'It came up during the night,' says the lady, who turned out to be a Miss Orsett.

"'Begging your pardon,' I said. 'It's come along, not up' – which it had, I knew, and I thought of it heaving its oozing self along in the dark while unknowing persons slept peacefully, not inches away. 'I'll speak to Father,' I said, but I knew it would be too late by the time he got there because I'd noticed, as she hadn't, that while we were stood there speaking it had come on a few inches. Time he arrived it would be on its way out, and at that moment it gave a kind of horrid ripple, all along itself, and little beads of moisture stood out, like sweat.

"'Did you see that?' Miss Orsett screeches, and clutches me.

"'Bomb damage, perhaps,' I said, on account of many structural defects that showed themselves long after the event. Not that we had any bombs, just here, but people do like a rational explanation.

"Well, come dinner time I told my dad, but he wasn't in any hurry to shift himself. He knew as well as I that, by now, it would have passed through.

"'Not that I won't go along later and have a word,' he said. 'Who lives next door to HER?'

"'It's empty,' I said, because I'd looked, specifically, knowing what was likely to happen. That afternoon Dad went back to Rutland Street and called on Miss Orsett, and like we'd expected, it had evacuated itself. He reckoned it would be morning before it showed up again, next-door-but-one to her, and asked very casually what was the name of the people there. I don't recall what it was, but when there came a thunderous knocking at half-past-eight next day, he said, 'That's them,' and he was all ready, with his cap on. But when he answered the door, there was Miss Orsett in a taking on the step.

"'It's come back!' she says.

"'What do you mean, it's come back?' he says.

"'It's coming down the wall in the parlour,' she says, so off we traipsed, her and me and my dad, and sure enough, in her front room, what we called parlours in those days, there it was again, hanging down behind the wallpaper like a huge human blister."

"HUMAN?" Mum said.

"Human-SIZED," Mr Mortimore said, "and those great groping hands going on ahead of it. And travelling downwards, like it was now, it didn't hang about. As we watched, it sort of probed around, blindly, and changed tack, off to the left.

"'It's going into the back room!' says Miss Orsett,

and so we nipped in there fast, and waited for it to come through, which it did after a while."

"Couldn't you stop it?" Eric said.

Mr Mortimore fixed him with a beady look. "How?"

"Burst the blister?" Eric said.

"And let it out?" Mr Mortimore said. "We thought about that. My dad says, to Miss Orsett, 'It looks like whatever it came for, it's got. You sure next door's empty?'

"'Well, there's furniture inside,' Miss Orsett says, 'but no one's living there, not since . . .' – and when she hesitated like that, we remembered. That house was the house of an acquitted man!"

"A what?"

"You've heard of convicted men?" Mr Mortimore said. "You've heard of condemned men? Well, this was an acquitted man. A long while back, at the start of the year, this mechanic from Cowley Road was found drowned down an old well in Hurst Street. Head down, he was, just his boot soles showing. There'd been a lot of ill feeling between him and his partner, and the partner was arrested and brought to trial. Faves, his name was; the Faves Case, got a lot of coverage in the national press, on account of the evidence which was thin, very thin, and he got off. Faves was the owner of the house next to Miss Orsett."

"You mean," Eric said, "that the damp patch was the mechanic come back for revenge?"

"Rose up out of the well and went searching for his killer," Mr Mortimore said. Then he said, "I don't know what I mean, to tell you the truth, but since we were all thinking along the same lines, Dad got a crowbar and broke into the house of Faves, next to Miss Orsett. Because," said Mr Mortimore, "we knew that Faves had done a bunk, so what had been going on?"

"What had?" Mum said.

"Oh, Doctor, when my dad forced that door and went up those stairs I was right behind him, with old Miss Orsett dithering on the pavement. Like she said, Faves had left some furniture behind, and in the front room upstairs there was a bedstead, and an old flock mattress, and on that mattress – " he looked at us, deciding whether or not we could take what was coming – "on that mattress was a bloated corpse, all pale and swelled, like it had been a week in the river. The first and last time," Mr Mortimore said, "that I ever saw a man drowned in his bed."

Mum said, "Drowned?"

"In bed?" I said.

"The inquest said pneumonia," Mr Mortimore said, "owing to the excessive fluid on the lungs. No mention was made of the fluid elsewhere."

Eric said, "Who was it?"

"It wasn't Faves," Mr Mortimore said. "We never knew for certain who, but when we checked the back door the lock had been smashed, so maybe some poor vagrant had come in, looking for shelter – on the wrong night. He got the wrong man!"

"Who did?"

"Who? What? I don't know," Mr Mortimore said, "but as we were coming out of there Mrs Minton's youngest comes up and says the wall's gone funny again.

"'Let it be,' says dad. 'It'll pass.' And it did. Never seen again, as far as I know, though I have heard there's an exceptional number of pneumonia cases reported in this area." He put down his cup, and went to look out of the kitchen door. "I wish I could remember," he said, "which house it was."

"Well, if it wasn't this one," said Mum, "it must have been the one at the other end, on the other side."

But we were all thinking. This is the Hurst Street end. And we thought of the well.

"Point is," Mr Mortimore said, "which is the one it'd be heading for, number seven this side or number eight the other? As far as I can see, Doctor, your damp patch is inert, but watch it. Watch it. If the weather stays wet, watch it very carefully. It's your social duty. If it got the wrong man last time, who's to say but it's still searching?"

That was last week. It hasn't rained since, but there's a storm forecast for tonight. We're watching. It's a funny way to spend Christmas.

Front

If you asked anyone today to name the Seven Wonders of the World they would probably start with
Disneyland and then stick. When I was at school we
knew them all: the pyramids of Egypt, the Pharos of
Alexandria, the Temple of Diana at Ephesus, the
Statue of Zeus at Olympia, the tomb of Mausolus at
Halicarnassus, the Colossus of Rhodes and the Hanging Gardens of Babylon. We also knew that, apart
from the pyramids, they no longer existed, so we
could only guess at what they had looked like. It
struck me that they were certainly huge, and that
was why they had been wonderful; early civilizations
had been just as prone as we are to admire things
because they are enormous: New York's World Trade
Centre, the CN Tower in Toronto. All except the
Hanging Gardens of Babylon; nothing was said about
the size of those and I thought I knew what they
looked like, at any rate. They looked like Rockingham Crescent.

The Crescent was a terrace of three-storey houses
on top of our hill. We lived five streets down, far
enough down for even the attics of The Crescent to be
invisible from our attic, and for years I did not know
it was there. I heard of it. "Oh, so-and-so lives in The
Crescent," grown-ups remarked, but so-and-so was
never anyone we visited and it was not on the way to
any of the places we did visit; school, the shops, the
cinema, the park. Only when I was given a bicycle

37

and went in for uphill endurance tests did I discover that The Crescent was not some distant, unattainable El Dorado but simply the road at the top of the hill.

Purple-faced, standing on the pedals, I did not know I had reached it until, labouring up Stanley Street, I discovered that the road had turned sharp right and levelled out. I dismounted and stayed where I was, leaning on the handlebars, head down, trying to breathe again without being sick. Stanley Street was 1 in 5 and the houses went down in steps, each lower than the last. I'd never noticed this before because, from the corner of our street, which was quite near the bottom, I'd only ever looked up. The Stanley Street houses stopped short of the hill top and on the right was an open grassy space that looked as if it were mown only rarely and ended in an abrupt lip where the hill dropped away below it. On the left was The Crescent – I identified it by the ancient iron street sign – and as soon as I saw it I knew that I had found the Gardens of Babylon.

It was a very shallow curve but it rose up like a cliff face. I had seen cliffs at Dover, white from a distance, but the closer you got, the greyer they seemed, grey and green where vegetation had sprung in cracks and on ledges. The Crescent was the same. The houses were faced with peeling stucco, white, grey, cream, but the stucco was hardly visible for every house was draped in vines; clematis, wisteria, jasmine, rambling roses, ivies and creepers, cascades of greenery, torrents of it, round windows, over doors, down into the areas below the pavement, interrupted here and there by a streak of red or white; a window box or a basket of petunias and pelargoniums. I knew enough about plants to realize that in fact it was all growing *up*, not down, but the impression was of a riotous tumbling; hanging gardens.

It was a summer afternoon. The sun shone full on The Crescent; the air was quite still. So far above the town it was silent, too. The whole place was transfixed, a mirage, until a sudden murmur of wind set every leaf and tendril quivering, as if the entire terrace had unanimously shuddered. Then it was still again.

To think that all this was here, had always been here, not 300 yards from our house. There was no one in the street but me. No one left a house or entered. No face appeared at a window, or hand twitched a curtain; no voice, no music; even the birds that sang sounded very far away. Reluctant to break the enchantment I stayed where I was, still clinging to the handlegrips and gazing up at the hanging gardens, but I knew that somehow I had to leave; I must make myself leave.

My other major birthday present was a wristwatch. I looked at it unwillingly. It was half past three. I was not expected home until five, for tea, and our home was barely one minute away by bike. Almost I was disappointed. I did not want to leave but I wanted to be *forced* to leave, to have to tear myself away and drag home with many a backward glance. Finding that I had no need to go placed me in imminent danger of leaving without regret, of abandoning a place that had ceased to exert any hold over me. But telling myself that my mother would worry that I had been involved in an accident – it was my first day out on wheels – I turned the bicycle with one last lingering look at the hanging gardens, and began to coast back down Stanley Street with a heavy hand on the brake. It was my first experience of courting sorrow.

"I'll come back," I whispered, "tomorrow." But the next day I rode downhill, towards the town, to experiment with danger and traffic lights. I did not go back to The Crescent that day, nor the next. The longer I waited the better it would be when I did; there was always another day, and another. Weeks passed. I did not mention The Crescent to anyone, as if I had been trespassing and needed to conceal the fact, but I thought of it often with a thrill of nostalgia that grew more poignant the longer I stayed away from the austere silence of the hill top, the lush waterfalls of vines. I could have walked there in not much more than five minutes. I did not go back again for three years.

Patricia Coleman and I must have started at the High School the same term, but we were in the second year before we noticed each other and in the third before we became, briefly, friends. There was no reason why we should not have been, but we were in different classes and rarely met. Then, in the third year, we were put in the same set for maths, and sets, like death, cut across class barriers. It was by no means a meeting of twin souls; perhaps one of us loaned the other a protractor or we converged on the pencil sharpener at the same moment. When we found ourselves by chance together in the dinner queue, there was a reason to speak, some general comment on the quality of the food, possibly. At school we talked about the food in the way that adults talk about the weather; something to discuss among people who have nothing at all to say to each other. Eventually we lingered in the cloakroom and talked, until the duty prefect threw us out. That must have been it – the duty prefect's doing. We walked home together. Even so, it was a couple of weeks before we realized how close to each other we lived.

The school was at the south end of the town, on the road that ran straight through it, pausing to become the High Street for a short distance. Just where the shops began, the dry cleaners and newsagents and hairdressers that always seem to congregate and hang about on the approaches to towns, Patricia – it was Pat by now – would slow down and say, "I turn off, here." We then hovered on the corner, finishing the conversation which had lasted us from the school gate, something urgent and instantly forgettable, and then Pat would say, "See you tomorrow," or, on Fridays, "See you on Monday," and strike off to the right up a side street the name of which I never noticed. I assumed that this was the street she lived in. I walked on past the parade of shops, picked up the evening paper at the newsagent's and then I too turned right, up Stanley Street, across the end of Speke Avenue, by the pillar box, and right again into Livingstone Drive, which was ours. In all my life, except for that one voyage of discovery, I had never been further up the hill than Livingstone Drive.

After about a fortnight, as Pat and I stood on the corner taking our customary ten minutes to wind down the conversation, she said, "Are you expected?"

"Expected where?"

"At home."

"I am this evening. Mum and Dad are going out and I've got to baby-sit." My sister was ten; hardly a baby. "Why?"

"I thought you might like to come home for a bit."

Of all the things that Pat and I discussed walking back from school, our homes had never been mentioned. The friendship was a school thing, but I suppose we were now sufficiently warmed up to feel a faint curiosity about each other, and to wonder how each would measure up when confronted by the other's family. And so as soon as Pat said "I thought you might like to come home for a bit," I glanced involuntarily up that right-hand turning to look properly, for the first time, at the houses which lined it. Disappointingly, reassuringly, they were Victorian terraces, just like ours; red brick, terracotta facings, sash windows, grey slates capped by red ridge tiles, with comforting green and yellow privet hedges and low brick walls bounding the small front gardens. No gates, as in our street, as in most streets in Britain, I guess. The gates had gone in the war, for scrap, along with the iron railing that had once topped the brick walls, sawn off at the ankle leaving blunt black stumps. I should feel at home in such a house. I should not shine, or feel inferior; it was my proper place.

"Tomorrow, then?" Pat said. Tomorrow was Friday. "Come and have tea." This too was proper. In those days tea was a meal to be invited to, a meal at a table, with bread and butter.

"Where does she live?" my mother asked, when I said that I would be late home, and why.

"That road up by the fish shop."

It was actually a fish and chip shop. For a moment I thought the invitation was going to be vetoed. Could one be seen socializing with people who lived in a street with a fish and chip shop on the corner?

"She lives by the *fish* shop?"

"No, further up." At a respectable distance, I hoped to suggest. After all, my mother could hardly put a whole street out of bounds because of something right at the end of it. There was a pub at the far end of ours.

"Wellesley Road," my mother said, after thinking for a bit. "It's quite nice up there. What did you say her name was?"

"Pat Coleman."

"What does her father do?" This was not quite so snobbish as it sounds. My mother was trying to work out if the name Coleman meant anything to her; was

42

he Coleman the barber, Coleman the bank manager, Coleman the coalman?

"I don't know," I said. What I did know was that he was never mentioned. Mummy was spoken of a great deal, but not Daddy, although it was somehow understood that he existed. He wasn't dead. A fearful thought suddenly struck me; perhaps he was in jail; Coleman the burglar. But no, people from Wellesley Road didn't go to prison, any more than they did from Speke Avenue or Livingstone Drive. That kind of thing went on down on the council estate, so I was given to understand, after all, what could you expect . . .?

"Probably in business," my mother said, comfortingly; comforting herself. Business implied desks, secretaries, filing cabinets and, of course, money. None of this was said. "Perhaps you could ask her here, some time?"

I should have thought of that. One look at Pat would have reassured her. Pat was the most *medium* person I had ever met. She might have been assembled from a set of statistics; average height, average build, neither fat nor thin, fairish hair, fairish skin; always somewhere around the middle of the class lists, neither embarrassingly stupid nor insultingly clever – like me, really. That is why we were in the same set for maths. In lessons she always answered questions correctly but never volunteered suggestions. She was safe. One look at her, two minutes' conversation, would have told my mother that.

"Be home by six-thirty, then," she said, "before it gets dark." It wouldn't get dark till well after seven, but I inferred that I was being allowed quite desperate licence.

I felt rather daring, on Friday, turning right, past the fish shop, up Wellesley Road with Pat. I was pushing my bike with a text book spread across the handlebars, and we did our homework as we went. Although we were in different sets for French we found that we had been given exactly the same translation. The teacher would not have approved of the way we were doing it, but we gave it our full attention, so we were quite a long way up Wellesley Road before I noticed just how far we had come. I had dropped the French book, stopped while Pat went to pick it up, and looked back. The road had curved considerably, and steeply, and the High Street was out of sight.

"Do you live right at the end?" I said.

"No, round the corner," Pat said, dusting off the book. I looked up ahead and for the first time saw that were almost at the end of the road. A few yards on it turned at a sharp angle to the left, and there was nothing in front of us but some scrubby elder bushes and a couple of buddleia. Beyond them was the sky, and I realized that by a circuitous route we had come to the top of the hill, and at the same moment Pat said, "We live in Rockingham Crescent."

"Really? Right in it?" I wished I'd known beforehand, so that I could have told my mother, but what I chiefly felt was astonishment. After all these years of promising myself another visit – one day – here I was by chance about to see it again without any planning or forethought. In one minute, in thirty seconds, I should once more set eyes on the hanging gardens, and in the remaining fifteen seconds experienced joyful anticipation and great reluctance, both at the same time. Did I want to return like this, unready, in the wrong frame of mind? What was wrong about it? I felt obscurely that I *should* have prepared myself, but it was too late now, we were at the corner, turning it. Almost unwillingly, I looked.

Nothing had changed. Except that this time I was seeing it from the opposite end, the view was exactly as I remembered it. The houses were a little smaller, perhaps, but all houses were a little smaller, these days, the road narrower, but so was ours, the expanse of grass that faced the houses less green and more littered, but otherwise all, all the same.

The side of the end house was deep in Virginia Creeper, just turning red. The autumn sun was soft, slightly hazy, and as before shone full on to the arc of greenery, the hanging gardens. There were fewer baskets and window boxes, in fact there was none, but I put this down to the season. People were planting bulbs in their window boxes now, weren't they? They were in our street.

"Which one's yours?" I said.

"Second one," Pat said, "with the red door." I drew my eyes from the green sweep of The Crescent, which, from where we were walking, was foreshortened into one Niagara of vines, and turned to the house we were approaching. It did not disappoint me. Ivy swarmed over the wall of the area and up the steps to the front door where clematis took over and higher up gave place to the Virginia creeper that had come across from next door and paused to engulf the windows before continuing to the third house and beyond. The windows were so overgrown it was difficult to make out what shape they were, and the ivy had been allowed to crawl across the fanlight over the door. I tried to imagine how it would look from inside, and gave up, knowing that I was about to find out, for Pat was opening the door.

"What about my bike?"

"Oh, put it in the area, it'll be safe," Pat said. I thought she meant me to take it down the steps to the basement, but there was just room inside the gateless opening to stand a bicycle and a dustbin which was there already, belching richly from under a dented lid tipped on at an angle.

45

I parked the bike and pushed the lid back into place, meanwhile staring down into the area. What had I expected to see? A kind of plunge pool, perhaps, boiling with leaf and stem. Instead the steps went precipitously down into a sump of old prams, bicycle wheels, two more dustbins, tea chests, lath and plaster – part of a ceiling. Out of it emerged a door under the steps and a cracked window hung with a yellow net curtain and swags of cobweb more substantial than the curtains. A few ferns drooped out of crevices in the wall.

"Come on," said Pat, in the doorway. I followed her up the steps, but not before I had noticed the area of the next house, almost entirely occupied by a striped mattress.

Now I really was wondering what I should find inside. The hallway was dark and narrow; so was the one at home, but ours contained nothing more than a hallstand and a table for the telephone. This one was full of bicycles, standing two or three deep between the door and the stairs which rose steeply to a darker landing, uncarpeted.

"Mind the bikes," Pat said, redundantly. We had to sidle round them as they lounged there, pedals outthrust, handlebars akimbo, like a bunch of yobbos blocking the pavement outside Woolworth's. Pat was on her way upstairs and I went after her, risking one glance over the decaying banister to see what lay below, and then wished I hadn't. A doorway with no door stood beyond the stairs, and through it I could see a room with no floor. The joists were there but the boards had gone, and the skirting board had gone, the window frame too. Through the space where the glass had been, an ubiquitous buddleia leaned in and ivy had its fingers over the sill, ready to climb through.

I leaned unwisely outward to see further, the

banisters swayed spongily under my hand and there was a tearing sound as if the whole structure were about to come out by the roots. Accustomed to the dark now I looked back down the stairs. What little sunshine was dribbling in through the ivy-stifled fanlight fell upon the bicycles and I saw that they were skeletons: tyreless, saddleless, wheelless in one case, stripped clean and abandoned. I turned the corner to the landing and found it blocked by an unattached gas stove. Then Pat opened the door somewhere ahead and light spilled out, illuminating a second flight of stairs, little more than a ladder, with no risers, and another door with boards nailed across it.

"Come on," Pat said, beckoning, and I followed her into the room where the light was coming from.

It was at least a whole room, ceiling, window, floor intact. There was even a carpet, and it was furnished. At first sight it seemed to contain enough furniture for the whole house. By the window was an oak dining table and four chairs with red plush seats; jammed up against it a cretonne-covered settee whose two accomplice chairs stood knee to knee in front of the fireplace. The rest of the space was taken up by a sagging double bed and a kitchen cabinet. Everything was very clean and very old, from the balding candlewick bedspread to the sheepskin hearthrug which, glimpsed between the armchairs, had been worn down to the skin itself in places, leaving small outcrops of fleece upstanding like clumps of pallid moss.

"Shut the door," Pat said. She took off her school mac and hung it tidily behind the door. There were several other garments clustered there, like over-crowded bats, so I draped my blazer over the bedpost. Pat took our school bags and stacked them in the corner, out of the way. Space was at a premium.

"Do you want some tea?" she asked.

"Yes, please." We had become very formal and polite, as if we were making conversation in a public place.

"Sit down, then. It won't take long."

I sat on the sofa. Pat made the tea. In a way, this did not take long because it was calculated to the point of maximum efficiency, given the parameters, as we say now. From a cardboard box in the hearth, she took a sheet of newspaper and a bundle of sticks. Even with my limited knowledge of building materials I recognized lath and split floorboard, although I had learned to recognize them only in the last ten minutes.

"I'm quite warm," I said. It was early October, very mild, and the room itself, with the window shut, was not only warm but stuffy. Pat took no notice. She crumpled the newspaper into the grate, built a tent of wood over it, set a match to the pyre and sat back on her heels to watch it ignite, now and then adding another stick of wood, strategically positioned. When it was burning well she laid on three lumps of coal, curious compressed things called Betteshanger nuts, and stood up.

"Keep an eye on it, will you?" she said, casually. "I'm just going to get some water." From the top of the kitchen cabinet she took down a black iron saucepan, wiped the inside with a teatowel, and went out. For a while I remained where I was, on the sofa, listening to her footsteps on the stairs; then I got up, crossed the room – in three strides – and looked into the cabinet. In the top cupboard was crockery, white, thick stuff, and a jug full of knives and forks. The bottom cupboard contained a flat iron, a dustpan and brush and a shoe box full of cleaning equipment: dusters, polish, Brillo pads, detergent. I closed the doors, listened for Pat returning, and hearing nothing lowered the flap in the middle. That section was the larder. It held a packet of tea, a bowl of sugar, a half pound block of margarine, a jar of mixed fruit jam, half a sliced loaf, the slices curling stiffly, and a bottle of milk. I began to understand. The kitchen cabinet was the kitchen.

There was still no sound of Pat's return. The room possessed one other door, almost obscured by the table and chairs. But there was just enough space to open it, and I did. What lay behind was obviously a cupboard, except that there was a bed in it, a camp bed with rickety crossed legs and covered by a grey army blanket. At that moment I heard a noise on the stairs, pushed the door to and hurled myself down in front of the fire, blowing industriously on it just in time, as Pat came in with the saucepan.

"Oh, thanks," she said, in that same casual tone. I moved aside and she put the saucepan on the fire, balancing it on the three Betteshanger nuts, as if on a trivet. Then, "Shall we finish our French while it boils?"

She dug the text book out of her bag and we sat on either end of the sofa, doing our homework. Occasionally Pat looked critically at the fire and added another Betteshanger nut. I kept wondering where the water had come from. It was becoming painfully apparent that this was Pat's home, all of it; this one room and the adjoining cupboard. Was there a bathroom? I wanted to go to the lavatory but dare not ask, for fear of what I should find.

After about half an hour the saucepan, which had no lid, began to steam. Pat arose and lowered the flap of the kitchen cabinet, laying out milk jug, tea pot, cups, saucers, and surreptitiously sniffing the milk bottle.

"Do you take sugar?"

"One spoonful, please." We might have been duch-

49

esses, so painfully correct were we. Pat measured one spoonful into each cup and one spoonful of tea into the pot. A faint agitation was discernible round the sides of the saucepan. My mother's insistence of a warm pot and boiling water came to mind, but it was already getting on for five o'clock. If we wasted any of that precious water warming the pot, if we waited for it to come to the boil, I might have to leave before tea was served, as Pat was well aware. The saucepan had barely begun to hiss before she emptied it into the teapot, which she stood in the hearth, in the hope of catching any extra heat that was going.

We took our tea to the table, perched uncomfortably on the red plush seats of the dining chairs. A plate of biscuits had appeared, the kind called Rich Tea, which always left me wondering what Plain Tea could be like. There were four. We took one each, tacitly acknowledging that to have more than that would constitute a serious breach of etiquette.

"I've got some biscuits in my room," Pat had said, dodging into the cupboard. She did not know I knew it was a cupboard. I did not say, "Oh, can I see your room?"

"Have you lived here long?" I asked, beginning to comprehend why my mother and her acquaintances communicated in such idiotic platitudes. It was not that they had nothing to say to each other, but there was so much that they could not, dare not say.

"About two years," Pat said, stirring her tea. I'd had first go of the spoon. Now that Pat had it she hung on to it, waving it about like a lorgnette to lend social poise to the conversation. When talk flagged she stirred her tea, vigorously. It had to last. Our two cups had emptied the pot; the pot had emptied the saucepan.

"Do you know, I live just round the corner, in Livingstone Drive, and this is only the second time I've been up here."

"Up where?"

"The Crescent. I came up here once on my bike."

"There's a marvellous view up here," Pat said. "At the front," she added.

She was too late. In my hurried prying while she was out of the room, I had not got around to looking out of the window. Now I leaned back and twitched the curtain aside to see what lay behind The Crescent, and immediately regretted it. At the back of the houses lay a fan of rubble-strewn gardens, collapsed brick walls, corrugated iron sheeting, elder, fireweed, wild hops and the ever-present buddleia. At the end of each garden was a small brick shed with, and in some cases without, a slate roof. The one at the end of Pat's garden had its roof and showed some signs of use, for there was a path beaten to it through the long grass and fireweed. Now I thought I knew where the lavatory was.

"We'll be moving soon," Pat said.

"Will you? Where?"

"Back to London, probably. Mummy doesn't really like it down here."

"Down here", I imagined, meant the Medway Towns, as opposed to "up here" which was The Crescent. Born and bred in the Medway Towns I felt a stir of protective indignation. What right had anyone to find fault with "down here", particularly someone who lived "up here"?

"Why did you come, then?" I asked, tactlessly.

"Oh, Daddy's work, you know." She looked me squarely in the eyes and tapped her knuckles with the tea spoon, daring me to commit another solecism by asking what, exactly, Daddy's work was. I had already been giving fast and furious thought to the problem of what to tell my mother when I got home. She would be full of questions about the household; she always was, trying to fit new acquaintances into

51

the complex structure of her social fabric. When we turned the corner at the top of Wellesley Road I had thought all would be well. I could tell my mother that Pat Coleman lived in The Crescent and our friendship would be encouraged. It had crossed my mind, after seeing the area, that it might be prudent to gloss over which particular house Pat lived in ("I didn't notice the number, honestly, Mummy . . .") but one look at those back gardens made me realize that it wouldn't matter which house I named, it would be all the same. The whole of Rockingham Crescent was the same, and I knew what my mother would call it; a slum.

Here at the rear of the house, out of reach of the sunshine, the room was growing dim. A pale square floated above the fireplace, the lowering sun reflected off a pane of glass somewhere out in that wilderness at the back. The fire glowed dull and smoky.

"Shall we put the light on?" I asked, without thinking.

"Oh, no," Pat said, quickly. "It's nice sitting here in the firelight." She seemed to speak of cosy winter evenings, logs, roaring flames, thick curtains drawn against the dark; not this dingy indoor twilight and the smouldering Betteshanger nuts. It was still light outside, and it was silent.

I lived in a terraced house. Not that we had noisy neighbours but you knew there were people on either side, next door but one, further up the road. There were voices, shouts, radios playing, cars starting up, dustbins clashing. Here in The Crescent it was silent, the only sound the occasional sighing of the fire, a creak as the coal shifted. Admittedly we were high above the town, but even so . . . not a dog barked.

At last we had to admit that we had finished our tea.

"I'll just clear all this up before Mummy gets back," Pat said.

Where was Mummy? "Shall I help?" I said.

"Oh, no." She gave a little laugh. "It won't take a minute."

She put the milk and biscuits into the cabinet, stacked the cups and saucers and teapot on to the breadboard and went out of the room. I stayed at the table, half inclined to follow and see where she did the washing up, half relieved that I wasn't going to find out. But it was a malicious impulse that made me get up, cross the room and press the light switch. There was a bulb with a fringed shade hanging at one end of the room, but it did not light up. There was a table lamp on the mantelpiece, plugged in at the wall. I pressed that switch too. Pat enjoyed sitting in the twilight because the electricity was turned off; and so was the gas, no doubt. The disconnected stove was on the landing. I opened the door and stood outside, by the stove, listening. From far away, down below, I caught the clatter of crockery and became aware of a vibrant hissing that seemed to rattle the bones of the house. Pat was washing up in cold water, straight from the main. Had that involved certain judicious adjustments to the stopcock in the street? When I heard her footsteps returning I dodged back inside again and was back at the table when she came in.

"What time did you say you had to be home?" she asked, stacking the cups and saucers into the top of the cabinet.

"Six-thirty."

"It must be nearly that now."

It felt as if I had been there for several hours, but we both knew it was no later than five-forty. A bedside clock with a domineering tick stood on the window sill.

"Yes. I'd better be going." I looked round for my bag and at the same time we both jumped. A door had slammed downstairs. I had jumped because I was long past expecting to hear any evidence of life, but Pat looked seriously alarmed. There were footsteps on the stairs.

I was shrugging on my raincoat and did not notice, at first, till I looked up and saw her holding out my bag, eyes staring, mouth open, hopelessly urgent. Hopelessly, because the footsteps were now dragging along the landing. The door opened and a woman came in, and behind her a child, a little boy of about five. The boy looked tired, the woman looked exhausted, beyond mere tiredness. She wore a head-scarf, scuffed suede boots and, in between, an ugly gingery coat with bristles rather than a nap. I had seen her before. I recognized the coat. I had seen her a dozen times, walking down Stanley Street, waiting in the Post Office, queuing in the fish shop; and I had seen her before a thousand times. She was every refugee, in every newsreel, in every war film, dressed in the only clothes she owned, all character erased from her face by the same blow that had smashed all hope, all resilience.

She looked at me and that beaten face did not alter in any degree, but from somewhere she found a voice.

"Why, Patsy, is this a school friend?"

And she turned to me, holding out a claw that my grandmother would have disowned. I suppose she was thirty-five at most. "How do you do?"

If my mother had heard her on the telephone she would have reported, "Very well-spoken." She was well-spoken, like Pat, a quiet respectable voice with no particular accent.

I took the claw and shook it. "How do you do?" I said, as I would have said it to anyone. "I'm sorry I've got to go. My mother's expecting me."

54

"Yes, it is getting dark," said Mrs Coleman. It was certainly getting dark in the room and Stygian on the landing.

"I'll see you on Monday," Pat said, as she always did on Friday evenings.

"Yes. Don't come down. I'll see myself out."

The door closed behind me and immediately Pat's mother said to Pat, "Oh, how could you? How *could* you?"

"She's my friend," Pat said, woodenly. I was manoeuvring round the gas stove at the time.

"But to bring anyone to *this* place . . ."

I was on the stairs.

"Doesn't look as if there'll ever be any other place," Pat said, without rancour.

"You lit the fire!" The voice was anguished now. "Oh Christ, that's the last of the coal."

I was in such a hurry to get away I almost forgot my bicycle parked in the area and had to go back for it. That slowed me down. In any case, I was in no hurry to go home; I had a story to concoct, after all, so I wheeled the bike along The Crescent, looking up at the houses as I went. And now I saw. The Crescent was derelict, every window boarded up, paint peeling, stucco crumbling, the areas choked with refuse. From the corner of Stanley Street at the top of the hill, where I had first seen them, I looked back and saw again the Hanging Gardens of Babylon, just as I had on that summer afternoon three years ago.

"You're early," my mother said. "Anything wrong?"

"I've got a lot of homework," I said.

"Did you have a nice time?"

"Yes. Huge tea." I was so hungry I felt sick.

"Is it a nice house?" How loaded is that word 'nice'.

"Lovely. Right at the top of the hill. I came back along Rockingham Crescent. Doesn't anyone live there now?"

"No one's lived there for a couple of years," my mother said. "It's condemned. A shame, really. They must have been lovely houses once."

Condemned. That word has made me feel ill ever since. I should never have gone back. The Hanging Gardens must have been near their end that first time I set eyes on them. I never went there again. Pat and I were not *that* friendly, not afterwards, and that was none of my doing although I was relieved by her coolness subsequently. I wouldn't have understood how to proceed, knowing what I knew, but she didn't seem to expect it.

"They moved," I said, when my mother proposed a return visit. "They were just about to move when I went there. All their stuff was packed." It was several years before I learned to admire Patricia Coleman, even if she had used me as an accessory, for exercising her right to ask a friend home to tea, like anyone else.

Closer than a Brother

Templeton I was hailed as a technological break-through when it first came out, but it did not break through in our house. We did not have one because Mick and Lesley said it would be a waste of money. This is standard Parent-speak for anything costing more than five pounds that they do not want to use themselves (e.g. video recorders were a waste of money until Lesley enrolled with the Open University) but in the case of Templeton I they were right. It had a multi-functional keyboard – which was fine if you had multi-functional fingers – and was about the size of a large-format paperback, which was fine if you wanted to nick one, only it was generally considered not worth nicking; in our house, anyway. Mick said it would be wiser to wait for the next model which would be Something Else and Lesley backed him up, so I was outvoted 2–1 as always.

Whatever the economic advantages of being an only child, remember – you will always be outnumbered. It is best to start hinting about a little brother or sister when you are three so that by the time you are my age your confederate will still be small enough to duff-up but also old enough to understand that it is always best to throw in one's lot with Big Brother. Not many three-year-olds realize this, though. I didn't, for instance. Still, where computers are concerned I usually bow to Lesley and Mick because they have *both* been working on mainframes

57

for many millions of years. I agreed (ho ho) to wait for Templeton II.

Mick was right. Templeton II was Something Else. It was the size of a portable typewriter – well, you don't need me to describe it. Everyone knows what a Templeton II looks like, remember the advertising campaign? Our Templeton II was a little different, but not where it showed, and I suppose it was the same as all the rest, to begin with.

Ours has its own room. I said it could share mine, but Lesley said it was not a *toy*. The little dining room next to the kitchen became the computer room and that's where Templeton II was lodged, all by itself, with its own table, desk and monitor. Rather like me upstairs, really, with my own table, desk and cassette recorder. Templeton II had its own cassette recorder too.

Templeton II was allowed about three months to settle in before Lesley decided that it was time it started earning its keep. I don't know what she and Mick were doing with it during that time, running IQ tests, I expect, and making it do press-ups, but I only played with it. I was younger, then. Everyone in my class had some kind of machine at home; they played games on them and I played games on ours. Templeton II came equipped with an introductory tape that showed some of the things it could do, in four colours, very slowly. It was like watching pages from Ceefax on a wet afternoon, waiting for Templeton II to finish drawing a pattern, and watching pages from Ceefax is the technological equivalent of watching grass grow. It was another matter when Templeton II started watching pages from Ceefax – but I'll get on to that later.

As I said, Templeton's childhood lasted three months, those happy days when we used to play games together, then it had to grow up fast and work for its living. Little did it know that its days of drawing patterns and making silly noises were numbered. I can still remember when I was at that stage and thought it would last forever, then on my fifth birthday Lesley and Mick bought me a little leather satchel (this was in the Dark Ages, mind you) and two weeks later I enrolled at the Wilfred Babcock Junior Mixed Infant School, as a mixed infant. Templeton II did not get a leather satchel. Templeton II got disc drive. That was the end of *his* childhood.

What am I saying? *It's* childhood.

When I went to school I had to start memorizing things: letters, words, numbers, tables. Templeton's memory started to fill up, too: phone numbers, addresses, dates, Open University data, but worse was to come. Interface.

At first I thought an interface was something you could actually buy, like an integrated circuit, but it wasn't so simple as that. Interface, it turned out, wasn't so much a thing as a happening. Templeton II was already fed to the back teeth with information then, hey presto, an interface! He had to start using it.

It was an awesome responsibility for an inexperienced machine but, as Mick said, when he switched from giving me pocket money to an annual allowance which meant that I had to open a bank account and keep records, no privilege without responsibility. Overnight Templeton II became near as dammit responsible for household security. There had been a lot of burglaries in the neighbourhood (all those micros and videos, no doubt) and people down our street were having burglar alarms fitted, or else just putting a dummy alarm on the wall to deter villains. Like putting a scarecrow in a field, this assumes the existence of some very dumb birds. There were horror stories about the Mackenzies round the corner who installed an incredibly sophisticated alarm system that automatically alerted the police station when it was triggered. Curtains for any burglar, of course, only it didn't take into account the Mackenzies themselves who, brainwise, have about one memory bank between the six of them. Every morning one Mackenzie or another would fling open the back door to take in great life-enhancing gulps of Putney air and forget to switch off the alarm first. Then there was a mad scramble to reach the telephone within thirty seconds or else a personnel carrier filled with SW15's finest unloaded at the gate.

Nothing like that for us. Templeton II was going to do the lot. First of all he was hooked up to the lights through his user port (this sounds painful but is all quite in order, in fact, it is his interface), no small undertaking for a machine the size of a portable typewriter. We have eleven rooms on three floors; that is a lot of lights if you include also the front hall, the back hall, the lobby, the landings, the porch and the downstairs loo. Templeton didn't get all of them (Mick wasn't up to rewiring the whole house) but he got more than he bargained for.

My education doesn't stop at school – according to Lesley it doesn't even *start* there – and we are out most evenings at the theatre, or a concert, or one of those small cinemas where they show films with subtitles that you don't get at the ABC Putney High Street; Mick and Lesley having a good time and me getting educated. During the burglary boom, which shows no signs of going into a slump round here although you'd think that everything worth nicking must have been nicked, people took to leaving lights on when they were out, usually on the landing.

It doesn't take your average burglar long to work out that your average family doesn't spend six hours a night sitting on the landing and in he goes, zap, pow, video shmideo. Not in our house. As soon as it began to get dark Templeton II woke up and started his night shift. First of all he switched on the light in the hall and the strips in the kitchen. Ten minutes later the living room would light up, *then* the landing, followed by my bedroom. By now the living room light was off again and stayed off for an hour, in which time my light went off, Mick and Lesley's room had lit up a couple of times and the kitchen had gone dark.

It stayed dark till ten, then lighted up again, along with the bathroom; the bathroom went off but the living room stayed lit till we came home from our culture trip. The really ingenious touch was the downstairs loo which lit up for two minutes randomly all through the evening. Mick, would you believe, actually timed the average slash.

"That doesn't account for people like you reading in there for half an hour at a time," Lesley said. Mick retorted that the average burglar wouldn't think of that. The average burglar, you see, was all this time hiding in the hedge opposite, waiting for us to vacate the premises. Ha! Little did he know that the premises were vacated all along, and that this frantic activity, upstairs, downstairs and even in the khazi, was the work of one man – one *machine*. After a few nights of chilly vigil he'd chuck it in and do the Bradleys instead, next door but two.

Soon after this the neighbourhood began to attract a better class of burglar; above average. You can imagine the type . . .

"And our first contender this evening is Mr Sid Shifty from Isleworth. And what do you do for a living, Mr Shifty?"

"I'm a burglar."

"At the end of that round, Mr Shifty, you scored thirteen points. You passed on four – "

"It's a fair cop, Guv."

This kind, apparently, is good with locks. Our front door was already fitted with something that looked as if it might detonate a controlled explosion and Lesley was always double-locking it by accident so that no one inside could get out. Templeton II to the rescue again. These days we do not have a lock on the outside. These days we have to stand in the porch and press buttons to feed in our personal identification number. When Templeton II is satisfied that it is 6259, 1712 or 3428 (me, Mick and Lesley) and not the above-average Mr Shifty, he releases the latch and the door opens. This is not foolproof. 1712 is always typing in his cash till number by mistake and then there was the occasion of the Great Power Failure. Ninety minutes it took us to effect an entry, at 11.15 of a February evening.

"Why don't you go out in the road and flag down a passing burglar?" Lesley said, nastily, but Mick climbed over next door's wall, Sellotaped up the pantry window and smashed it with a brick. (I sometimes wonder how come he is so well informed about burglars, I mean, who takes Sellotape to *Much Ado about Nothing?*)

It was around this time we got a Teletext adapter, which only a few months before would have been a Waste of Money, and after that Templeton II began to help with the shopping. If Mick or Lesley fancied a particular component for Templeton they turned up Hutchinson's Electronics on Ceefax and Templeton ordered it from Hutchinson's own computer, quoting Mick's or Lesley's credit card number. By four o'clock that very afternoon, the order was dispatched. Lesley said that if we lived in Milton Keynes we could order the groceries that way as well instead of shlepping them back from Sainsbury's. I don't know why we haven't moved to Milton Keynes, to tell you the truth;

it sounds just about the same as living in a mainframe.

All this meant that Templeton II had to learn how to use the telephone. When *we* got the Teletext adapter *he* got a modem. This is the middle man, wired in between Templeton II and the telephone, so for convenience – *his* convenience of course – we had to move the telephone into the computer room. Lesley had an extension installed in the hall for the rest of us. Also, someone took out a subscription to *Tempo*, which is the Templeton users' mag, and with the aid of this Mick taught Templeton to play the piano, one of the privileges that go with responsibility. I used to sit up in my room and listen to Templeton, down below, playing ragtime while Mick joined in on his fiddle. Once upon a time he'd hoped to teach me to play the piano but I have a tin ear. You'd think that if anyone had a tin ear it would be the computer, wouldn't you?

Templeton II did not have an actual piano, you understand; he had a synthesizer chip, from Hutchinson's, connected through his user port via a length of that rainbow-coloured ribbon cable; and although he was playing piano rags, come to think of it he sounded more like a small fairground organ. Before long, Mick had stored *all* of Scott Joplin's rags on floppy disc, so that Templeton could accompany his fiddling. I rather hoped we would get a voice chip and teach him – it – to sing.

One night we came home from the Festival Hall and were waylaid on the front path by Mrs Sanderson from next door. It was nearly midnight and she was wearing a dressing gown.

"For crying out loud," said Mrs Sanderson, "I didn't know you were out. I thought you must all be dead. I've been ringing and ringing."

"I'm sorry," Lesley said. None of us knew what Mrs

63

Sanderson was getting at. "I thought I'd explained about the lights."

"Who's complaining about the lights?"

"I mean, it looks as if we're in when we're out," Lesley explained helpfully.

"If you're out," Mrs S demanded, "who's playing the organ?"

"How can we be playing the organ if we're dead?" I said, and Mrs Sanderson gave me a filthy look – I could tell, even in the dark.

"Come in here," she said. "Come in and listen." We followed her down *our* path, round the brick pillar between the gates and back down *her* path. As soon as we got inside her front door we knew what she meant. On the other side of the wall someone was playing *Maple Leaf Rag*, fortissimo.

We all looked at each other. "It's the computer," Mick said, lamely.

"I don't care what it is," cried Mrs Sanderson. "Since half past seven – "

"At that volume?"

"It's got louder and louder."

"Wait here," Mick said, and shot out of the door. Naturally I went with him, because if we had been visited by an above-average burglar with a mania for electronics *and* Scott Joplin, I wanted to meet him, but no go. As soon as Mick reached our porch and typed in 1712 the music stopped. Dead. We rushed down the hall and into the computer room but it was dark and all was silent. There was no burglar of any description, anywhere in the house. Nothing was disturbed and nothing was missing. Templeton II switched on the lavatory light a couple of times while we were searching, and the living room suddenly went dark, which was unnerving, but that was all. After a bit we heard Lesley and Mrs Sanderson creeping round to see if we'd been done in by the burglar.

"No burglar," Mick said.

"But why leave the computer playing ragtime if you're going out?" Mrs Sanderson demanded. Lesley murmured things about malfunctions and *grovelled* apologies, and Mick offered her a drink. I went up to my room, partly so that I wouldn't have to see Mrs Sanderson drinking brandy in her dressing gown – that sort of experience could stunt your growth – and partly to do a bit of quiet thinking. We had gone out at five past seven. Twenty-five minutes later something had activated Templeton II and he had gone into his ragtime routine.

It's the kind of thing I do myself. On the rare occasions when Mick and Lesley go out without me, I batten down the hatches, lay in a supply of canned tooth-rot, crisps, etc, and let rip with the hi-fi. But that's the point; the hi-fi is in the living room, on the far side of the house (which is semi-detached) not up against Mrs Sanderson's party wall, like my bedroom or the computer room. Of course, Templeton II wasn't to know about the party wall, but then, Templeton II wasn't supposed to know anything he hadn't been told, and no one had told him, "Look, TT, everyone's out. The house is empty. Enjoy yourself while you can." *He'd worked it out.*

He had worked out that he was required to operate the lights only when there was no one at home to do it. He had worked out that if he started a jam session while we were there to hear him, there would be questions asked and possibly some punitive action with the pliers. He had worked out, therefore, that if he was on lighting detail the coast was clear and he could hit the ragtime in a big way until one of us punched in our number at the front door. From 7.05 am onwards he could do as he liked, although he'd obviously allowed us twenty-five minutes to get clear. His only mistake was in turning up the volume.

Mick and Lesley went on for ages about malfunctions which I thought was pretty naïve of them as they always belch smoke and fire when people blame huge telephone bills and dodgy rate demands on a computer hiccough. I didn't say anything, but I began to wonder about all the other things Templeton II might get up to when the house was empty. What do *I* do when the house is empty, for instance? It was thinking about telephone bills that gave me a lead.

Well, what do *you* do when the house is empty, especially in the absence of the aforementioned little brothers and sisters to duff-up and sing nursery rhymes to? Yes. So do I. Just like Matilda in the poem I go tiptoe to the telephone and ring up all my dear friends. I don't get the chance all that often, but when I do, I take it.

The phone bill that quarter was astronomical. (Parent-speak again; it was larger than usual.) I got the blame, naturally. Who else would be making calls on the quiet? Detective work was called for and a bit of intellectual planning. It was quite clear that Templeton II never did anything he shouldn't when we were in the house, but how could he tell when we weren't? If he had to work the lights in the evening it was obvious, but how did he know that the place was empty during the daytime? He might count us out as the front door opened and shut, but sometimes two of us went out together. The phone had to be the answer. If no one answered the phone then the house was empty, but that would only work if someone rang up and he monitored the call. Suppose no one rang up? I tricked him.

One day I manoeuvred myself into being the last out of the house, having first opened the kitchen window. Then I nipped round to the back, over next door's wall again (they were all at work) and indoors via the sink, unobserved by Templeton II. There was no way he could have observed me, really, unless I'd made him open the front door, but as it turned out he was far too busy to notice me, even if he'd had ears, eyes and ESP. I crept into the computer room and came up behind him. As far as I could see he wasn't doing anything, but then it's difficult to tell if a computer is doing anything anyway; your average home micro is not precisely a get-up-and-goer. On the other hand, I was fairly sure he wasn't just sitting there. Then the phone rang. I belted into the hall.

My first instinct was to answer it, but of course, I realized, before it was too late, that this was probably Templeton's signal. The phone rang ten times and then stopped. This meant that either the caller had hung up, which seemed unlikely after thirty seconds, or Templeton had answered it himself. It was *then* that I lifted the receiver. Silence – well, a faint buzz. What passes for silence on a telephone line. But no voice, no breathing, no sound of someone putting the phone down at the other end . . . and then, as I stood there in the hall, clutching the handset like someone posing for a portrait, *Youth with Extension*, I remembered the last time this had happened. When the man came to install the extension he had a special number to dial which made the phone ring, so that he could test whether or not it was working. When he had gone I tried it out for myself, since I had been squinting over the engineer's shoulder when he dialled. Sure enough, our phone rang as soon as I replaced the handset. Up till then I'd only tried dialling our own number, which doesn't do the trick at all. I told Mick and Lesley, because we have quite a lot of trouble with our phone – who doesn't? – and I thought it would be useful if we knew how to test it. Mick put the number in his personal telephone directory which is stored, as I think I mentioned, in Templeton II.

And *that*, ladies and gentlemen, was how Templeton II discovered if the house was empty each morning. If no one answered the phone, it was all systems go.

I didn't know yet, though, which systems were going. I went back to the computer room and looked at Templeton. I wouldn't go so far as to say he looked busy, but he had an air of preoccupation, as though he were concentrating on something. I switched on his monitor. Templeton II was reading Ceefax – the pages listing electronic equipment sold by Hutchinson's.

"Who said you could do that?" I asked him, but of course, he didn't hear. I read over his shoulder, for a bit, and then I noticed that the red light was showing on his modem. Templeton was on the line again. I nipped out into the hall and lifted the receiver on the extension. All I could hear were high-pitched bleeps, but given his reading material I came to the conclusion that he was doing a spot of mail ordering and I was fairly sure this wasn't the first time. It would explain, for instance, why everyone had so vigorously denied taking out the subscription to *Tempo*, and why there had been such heated arguments between Mick and Lesley about who had ordered which integrated circuits.

"I won't shop you," I said softly and closed the kitchen window before leaving for school, but I went out through the front door. That made him jump, I bet.

I wasn't altogether surprised when, the following day, a jiffy bag arrived from Hutchinson's Electronics. It was addressed to Mr M Morrison, which is not me, but I slipped it into my pocket and opened it during break at school. Two minds with but a single thought; evidently I wasn't the only one who'd decided that it would be nice if Templeton II could have a voice chip, but he'd gone one better than me. I'd asked Mick and Mick had said, predictably, "Waste of money. We'll scc. Leave it for now," etc, etc. Templeton II hadn't bothered to ask but, being Templeton II, it hadn't occurred to him that getting it working meant relying on the goodwill of certain persons. I wasn't up to it and, bright though Templeton II was turning out to be, he was in no position to advise me.

I regret to say I lied. What would you have done? It was due to be Mick's birthday on 10 April, conveniently just after the start of the financial year. My allowance goes into the bank on 5 April, but the account is usually empty by the beginning of March and I have to con an advance out of Lesley. She says it's worth letting me have it for the fun of watching me working out plots to extort it from her, which is sadistic, I think. Anyway, I went to her with a yarn about ordering the voice chip for Mick's birthday present on *his* credit card, and begged her to cover up for me when the account was rendered. She wasn't amused this time, I can tell you, and she called me every kind of a crook and an idiot.

"Why didn't you use *my* credit card number?" she demanded. (What sort of parental guidance is that, I ask you?) I could hardly tell her the truth, could I? That it wasn't me who'd ordered the thing. I mean, I'd promised Templeton II not to grass on him, but I cursed him all the same. I wondered how to convince Templeton that this form of fraud may be what computers are good at, but only in multi-national companies. It doesn't work so well in a household of three people.

Well, we got away with it that time, though in the end it was Templeton II who blew his own cover. He got ambitious – but we didn't find out until the next phone bill came in. Meanwhile, Mick had his birthday. I wrapped up the chip in wads of cotton wool and tissue paper and a huge gift box that looked as if it might contain an inflated football. This is the kind of simple-minded joke that appeals to Mick and quite helped him get over the revelation, by Lesley, that she had told-Jonathan-he-could-order-it-on-*her*-credit-card-but-he'd-got-the-numbers-mixed-up. For she's a jolly good mother, etc. I bought her a whacking great bouquet of flowers on her birthday (with my money this time). She was a bit surprised as she is never quite sure if giving flowers to ladies is OK or sexist.

"Look, I'm your *son*," I reminded her. She blushed a bit, as though that small fact had escaped her memory.

This was a long while afterwards, though. Mick forgave me for the fraud – after I'd paid him back – and wired in the voice chip.

Templeton II didn't have a lot to say for himself, to begin with, and he had a terrible American accent, which none of us was prepared for. He is an *English* computer, after all, though if he'd broken out in Japanese we wouldn't have been too surprised. I bet Mick and Lesley were prouder of his first words than they were of mine, and he prattled away to himself like some sort of budgie. I wondered if he was as disappointed with the results as I was because it was about then that I understood why he wanted a voice. And it was about then that the phone bill arrived. This time it really was astronomical, it was intergalatic. Mick confronted me with it.

This is the only-child problem again. If your parents trust each other then, in situations like this, there is only one person left for them not to trust. Of course, Mick and Lesley were not to know that in this particular situation there were *two* candidates for the high-jump.

"Own up," said Mick, and his eyes were cold, like he'd left his contact lenses in the fridge overnight. "In order to run up a bill like this you would have to be calling the other side of the world, *every day*. All day, by the look of it."

"Who would *I* be ringing on the other side of the world?" I said, in a last-ditch attempt at stalling. "*When?*"

Lesley just clutched her head and moaned, "Nine hundred and eighty-seven pounds, fifty-six pence including VAT."

"Perhaps it was a computer hiccup?" I suggested unwisely. I really thought that for the first time in my life Mick was going to thump me, but it would have been against his principles and he controlled himself. Veins stood out on his forehead.

"Which computer?" he said, bitterly. "Bloody Templeton II, I suppose."

He thought he was making a heavy joke and it took me about half an hour to convince him that he was right.

"Look," said Mick, clinging to sanity by a thread, "all right, all right, suppose I accept that Templeton is ordering his own magazines and components. For all I know he's joined a computer dating agency. But that doesn't account for a thousand quid's worth of phone calls. *Where is he getting the numbers from?*"

"You," I said.

"Me?"

"Your personal directory."

"But those are mainly business contacts," Lesley said.

"Firms with computers?" I said.

"Most of them."

"Firms with computers on the other side of the world?"

We ran through the directory on Templeton's monitor. The numbers weren't quite on the other side of the world. The nearest was in Dublin. There were others in Lyons, Vienna, Zurich, Helsinki, Athens, Reykjavik and Lexington Massachusetts. They are the ones I can remember, at any rate – oh, yes, and Caracas and Tel Aviv. There were lots more.

I said, "He's just been ringing his friends."

It was a sticky moment for Templeton II. He nearly lost his interface there and then, but I leaped to his defence. I had to, didn't I?

"He's lonely," I said. "He's bored out of his skull, left on his own all day and most evenings. You've educated him and he's got nothing to do. He wants company."

"Don't be so sentimental," Mick snapped. "He's – it's – a computer."

"I don't care if he is," I shouted. "He's lonely. He's got nothing to do and no one to talk to. He's like me," I howled, going right over the top. "He's got no one to play with. I know how he feels!"

"So what do you suggest?" Lesley said. "We get him a friend?"

"Why not?" I said. "They can talk to each other. No more phone calls."

"They'll probably plot to take over the world between them," Mick said. "They'll hack into the Pentagon."

"*Two* computers?" Lesley said. "Sitting side by side like china cats?"

"You could put one of them in my room," I said. "They don't have to see each other, do they? They *can't* see each other. It's the communication that matters."

"Are you sure you didn't cook this up between you?" Mick said, suspiciously.

"Between who?"

"You and Templeton."

"I've learned to live alone," I said, with dignity. "It's him I'm thinking of."

"It," said Lesley, but without much conviction.

So now we have two computers, and Templeton is educating mine; I don't have much to do with it at all except dust it, but that wasn't the end of the affair by a long chalk. The end of it is only just beginning. Mick and Lesley really took it to heart when I said that I knew how it felt to have no one to play with or talk to and quite soon, within the next fortnight, I shall finally get that little brother or sister – centuries too late, of course, to be any use. It will quite likely grow up thinking I'm its uncle or its grandfather, and if I ever get round to playing with it, it will only be to see if it floats, or something like that. If she is a girl, she will be Annabel Lucy, and if he is a boy, he will be Sebastian Thomas, but for the time being I'm calling it Templeton III.

A Can of Worms

The desk, where the cash register stood, was probably the most valuable item in the shop, although wear and tear must be reducing its value daily. Every time the drawer of the cash register shot out, the desk legs jarred and a furtive click indicated that the left-hand cupboard had opened underneath.

Dora picked up the routine quickly, her fingers that had initially faltered over the keys skipping more surely with each transaction; price of each book, sub-total, cash tendered, total – the drawer opens, the cupboard opens, put in money, take out change, slam drawer, slam door. It would become an automatic sequence very soon, Dora guessed, when trade picked up and she had to serve one customer after another. At two o'clock, only half an hour since she began, people were still filtering in one at a time, and not all of them bought books.

"When does it start getting busy?" Dora said. Lou, the supervisor, looked down from her stepladder.

"Some days it doesn't," she said. "We aren't exactly W H Smith, are we?"

"It looks quite crowded, sometimes," Dora said.

"It doesn't take much to make a place this size look crowded." Lou climbed down the ladder, balancing gracefully with both arms full of books. As she set foot on the floor a little cloud of dust rose from the books and haloed her fluffy hair in the sunshine. "I shouldn't wear white too often, if I were you. Nothing collects dust like books."

Dora glanced down at her T-shirt.

"It's an old one."

"Sure," Lou said, "but it doesn't look too good if you go on the till after you've been in the basement. We have coffee at three and then change places. Jo – she's downstairs, sorting stock – will come up here, and I'll take you down and show you what she's been doing. Tomorrow you might be sorting first – that's the *really* dirty work."

"Shall I be doing that next?"

"No, I think I'll put you on shelving for now, looking round, seeing where the different categories are, finding gaps, bringing up replacements from downstairs. That way you learn where everything goes. We try to make sure that the shelves never look empty. People think we're running out of stock, which we aren't. You've seen what it's like in the basement."

The basement was the first thing Dora had seen when she dropped into the FreshWater bookshop and offered her services during the holidays. She passed it regularly, always looking in but never entering until today when she saw the poster in the window: *Volunteers wanted: can you help us?* When Mum had sent her out to find a job neither of them had considered voluntary help in a charity bookshop, but smarting from two rejections at supermarkets – "It's the eczema, dear" – Dora had decided that what she needed to feel at that moment was *wanted* and she began to feel wanted when she was directed to the basement and saw the voracious gleam in Lou's eye.

"Can you do Saturdays?" was the first thing Lou had said, even before she had climbed out from among the wobbling stacks of books, but then she had hesitated when she saw the scarlet patches on Dora's wrists. "Eczema? Won't the dust be a problem?"

"It doesn't weep," Dora had said.

"Well, you won't be down here all the time," Lou said, to Dora's relief. The low-ceilinged basement housed a cupboard with *Kitchen* on the door, a cupboard with *Cloakroom* on the door, and several thousand books.

At three o'clock Jo, who turned out to be an elderly-auntie type, came up to take over the cash register and Dora went below again. Lou was in the kitchen cupboard with a jug kettle and coffee jar; as Dora came through, Lou's arm snaked out in a dextrous manoeuvre and placed a steaming mug in her hand.

"How's it going?"

"Fine," Dora said. It was fine, sitting in the sunny window, watching people pass in the street, pause and look in at the display. One thing she'd learned very quickly was not to catch the eye of potential customers. She had smiled at some and they were the ones who smiled back, shifted their eyes and then passed by, feeling pressured.

The window display was made up of either very ancient books that looked as if they might be valuable ("If they were they wouldn't be here," Lou said) or very new ones with bright jackets. Down in the basement the new ones could be seen in all their minority, here and there among the ancients like the salad filling in a wholemeal sandwich.

"Do you sell all of them in the end?" Dora asked as they drank their coffee.

"Good Lord, no," Lou said. "They get three months on the shelves – look, they all have a date on the fly-leaf. If they haven't shifted by the sell-by date we reduce the price and put them in the bargain book-

case. The real no-hopers go for pulping – in there."
She kicked a large cardboard box. "Even that brings
in a bob or two, mainly hardback fiction. Nobody
seems to want that; they prefer paperbacks. You
probably noticed, we keep a big rack of those by the
door. Lures 'em in."

A young man with a beard skittered down the
stairs and shimmied between the dingy stalagmites
of books without dislodging any of them, like a blind
man showing off in the dark.

"You'll have the whole lot down one day," Lou said,
unimpressed. "Tony, this is Dora, joined us today.
Tony does our pricing."

"I'm the realist," Tony said. "No one ever made
money overestimating the public's generosity." He
smiled at Dora and turned right, into a dark cul-de-
sac beside the cloakroom, shucking off his jacket as
he went. Then the light came on and Dora saw what
he would be pricing. Like the rest of the basement
that corner was lined, floor to ceiling, with shelves,
but the floor was stacked with more cardboard boxes.
"That's the new stock," Lou said. "Tony sorts and
dates it and decides the price."

"What did he mean about overestimating the public's generosity?" Dora said. On the evidence of the
basement alone, the public seemed to be overwhelm-
ingly generous about donating books.

"You'd be surprised how many people try to beat
you down over the price," Lou said. "Everybody
thinks books are expensive, however little they cost.
And they nick them."

"From *here*?"

"Oh sure. If you look in that cupboard under the
desk you'll find a list of our regulars; the ones to look
out for. And you'd be surprised how many of these
are nicked in the first place. Schools, libraries . . .

people seem to have a moral gap when it comes to books."

"A *book* shop?" Mum said, when she went home that evening.

"A charity bookshop," Dora said, resolved to let the worst be known from the outset. "It's voluntary. I don't get paid."

"I know what voluntary means," Mum said. "I thought the whole purpose of this operation was to earn some money."

"That was your idea," Dora muttered. "I just wanted something to do."

"Very laudable, but I did suppose that remuneration would come into it somewhere."

"There wasn't anything," Dora said. "I tried three shops and they all wanted somebody permanent. I *won't* work in a burger joint – "

"Vegetarianism's turning out quite an expensive indulgence, isn't it?"

"Yes, well, we can afford it, can't we?" Dora said, sourly. "I don't blow my allowance in six weeks like John does. Anyway, I don't think they'd have me. The supermarkets wouldn't, not even for shelf-filling." She held out her blotchy hands. "Anyway, wouldn't you rather I was doing something really worthwhile than nothing at all? It's not for ever; only till September."

"Every day?" Mum sighed.

"Every afternoon," Dora said. "One-thirty till five."

"So perhaps you can find something that *pays* for the mornings?"

"I'll go on the game, if you like!" Dora said, slamming out of the room.

Gran was in the hall, tweaking a jar of delphiniums into shape. Dora would not have been so base as to assume that she was eavesdropping, but Gran, in her flimsy gold-stitched mules, was clearly neither going out of the house nor coming in, and the flower arranging looked suspiciously like a piece of stage business when someone has missed a cue.

"I suppose you heard that," Dora said, gracelessly.

"I still have my hearing and my teeth, thank the good Lord," said Gran, slipping into her old crone routine. It was hard to imagine anyone less like an old crone. At seventy-five Gran did not make the tactical and tactless error of supposing that she and Mum might be taken for sisters, but if she had claimed to be sixty no one would have doubted it. Her face was lined, but her immaculate blow wave was still more blonde than white, and her figure elegant rather than angular, her movements agile.

"Spry, dear," Gran said, when anyone remarked on this. "Not agile, not at my age. Old ladies are spry."

She gave the delphiniums an appraising look, over the bridge of her patrician nose, and turned to Dora. "I think I could carry off a coat that colour, this autumn," she said.

"What colour?"

"Delphinium blue. I could have my hair rinsed to match."

"Oh give it a rest, Gran."

"Claws in, darling. Whatever the row's about, I've no part in it."

"She thinks I ought to be earning for the good of my soul. What's the point of giving me an allowance and then expecting me to go out and earn more? I don't *need* more."

"Rosemary believes in the dignity of labour," Gran said, vaguely. "The Protestant Work Ethic, whatever that is."

"We're atheists."

"Yes, but *Protestant* atheists."

"I *am* working," Dora said. "Not getting paid for it doesn't make it less like work. I suppose the real reason is that I'll enjoy it. As far as Mum's concerned, work isn't work unless it makes you miserable."

"She's not really in a position to know, is she?" Gran said, with silky malice.

"This is really worthwhile," Dora said. "It's for charity, a Third World self-help project; sinking wells."

"You're going to sink wells, darling? How arduous."

"No, of course I'm not," Dora snapped.

"I didn't hear as much as you seem to think," Gran said. "Come upstairs and tell me *all*."

Gran had her own sitting room on the first floor, what would have been the most desirable bedroom, with a little iron balcony overlooking the street. She had furnished it herself, restfully, in white and shades of blue. If she did dress to match the delphiniums, she would merge with the upholstery, like a moth on a tree trunk.

"It's a second-hand book shop," Dora said, "down Lower Dukes Lane, between Culpepper's and the craft gallery."

"I thought that was the Trattoria Bologna?"

"It used to be. They've only been there a few months. It's the FreshWater Trust, the charity is, you know, like Oxfam and Help the Aged, only they just sell books and prints, only Lou says they don't get given many prints."

"And who is Lou?"

"She's the woman who runs it. All the staff are volunteers but she says they're always short-handed in the summer holidays. She's got this poster up in the window, asking for helpers. She almost *fell* on me when I said I could do Saturdays."

"And this is just Saturdays?"

"No, every afternoon. If Mum's really worried about the money, I'll go and wash up at the Duke's Head in the mornings," Dora said. "But I don't see why she should be. She can't pretend she thinks I should be earning my keep. She's always having to bail John out."

"I'll have a word," Gran said, superbly, indicating that a word from her was all that was needed. "Now let's have a gin and tonic to celebrate."

"Celebrate what?"

"Oh, I don't know . . . any excuse. We can drink to charity, fresh water, self-help – no, I'll make them. You're much too free with the tonic."

Dora watched Gran, still supple, stoop without effort to take out the glasses and bottles from her little sideboard that stood on the same bow legs as the desk in the shop. Gran was not at all free with the tonic, the main reason why Dora had been about to mix the drinks herself. Mum fretted discreetly about Gran's gin, and begged Dora not to encourage her, as if Dora smuggled it into the house after dark. Dora saw no reason why Gran should not get roaring drunk if she felt like it. If you couldn't do as you pleased at seventy-five, when could you let rip? You might as well die at thirty, a prospect that appealed increasingly to Dora. What was there left, after that?

Lower Dukes Lane sloped steeply from the modern shopping centre to the narrower streets of what remained of the medieval city round the cathedral. On Saturday afternoon Dora, who had been buying shoes, approached it from the upper end and stood for a moment, under her umbrella, gazing down towards FreshWater Books. The lane turned slightly to the right just there, and she could see into the shop for in the dull, rainy afternoon, Lou had switched on the lights, illuminating the shelves, the racks, the desk where she would shortly be sitting herself. At the moment the place was occupied by a woman in a red blouse, not Jo – Jo was fatter than that – and Lou had brown hair. Dora had a sudden vision of herself sitting at the desk, seen from a distance, seen by someone else standing under an umbrella in the rain and thinking, I *must* go in there.

She ran down the lane, which was paved but wide enough to admit delivery vans, closed the umbrella and entered the shop. There were several damp customers standing about on the green carpet tiles, but Lou, on a stepladder as usual, saw her at once and climbed down.

"You're early."

"Does it matter?"

"No, it's perfect. Susan – " she waved to the woman in red " – has got to go, and Paul's just rung to say he won't be in. Can you take over on the till for now? I know I said I'd put you on to shelving but, well, Saturdays are like that." She laughed apologetically.

"That's all right. I like it on the till."

"Most people think it's terribly boring."

"I can always look out of the window."

She took Susan's place at the desk and watched her, huddled into a white trench coat, hurry up Lower Dukes Lane, pause at the top where Dora had paused, and plunge away to the left, heading no doubt for the car park.

"Excuse me . . ."

Dora turned guiltily and saw a man standing at the desk, holding a pile of paperbacks.

"Holiday reading," he said. "Have you got a carrier bag?"

Dora nodded, smiled efficiently, madly trying to remember the sequence of keys on the cash register, getting it right but taken unawares when the desk door swung open and hit her knees.

"You get used to it," Lou said, stretching past her to prop up an open book with enticing colour plates, in the window display. "Actually, while it's open, you might as well read what's inside. I'm not sure that it does much good, but we can't just ignore it."

Dora stooped below the level of the desk and saw that taped to the inside of the cupboard door was a number of file cards, written out in different hands.

Short, middle-aged man. "City gent" clothes. Middle Eastern? Carries briefcase. Always pays for purchases but needs watching.

Elderly woman, tall, well dressed. Wears a grey cape. Never buys anything.

Tall youngish man, "down and out" appearance. Usually comes in about 4.15 and stays till closing time.

Teenage girl, dyed blonde hair, black jeans. DM boots. Has a friend with her, always a different friend. Friend usually buys something. A team?

"Our regulars," Lou said. "We've got the mirror, of course, but there aren't enough of us to keep watch all the time. The person who usually does spot something is on the till and you can't leave that to chase them up the road."

There was a list of regulations taped to the wall above the desk. The first one, in large type, read, NEVER LEAVE THE TILL!

"I mean," Lou said, "until they're out of the shop they technically haven't stolen anything, and by the time they're outside and you've called someone off the shelves or rung down to the basement, it's too late. Don't worry about it," she said, "but if you should recognize one of our chums, let us know. Don't feel you've got to stare at the mirror the whole time. It's as much a deterrent as anything."

All the same, Dora found herself paying rather closer attention to the convex mirror that hung in an angle at the back of the shop. With the lights on it was more obvious than it had been yesterday, but too distant to show more than the kind of view seen from the wrong end of a telescope; incredibly detailed but miniaturized beyond mortal eyesight.

At five to three another stranger came up from the basement, a young woman in dungarees. "Aline," she introduced herself. "You must be Dora. It's your coffee break – oh, hang on, I've got something for you. Nothing exciting, I'm afraid." She held out a badge identical to the one that she and Lou and the others wore, a white disc printed in blue with the word FRESHWATER and, inevitably, three wavy lines underneath.

"One of us," Aline said, affably; Dora pinned it on her sweater and went downstairs to Lou and coffee in the basement, one of them.

"You've had a good day, I can tell," Gran said, when Dora came in, shaking water from her hair, having left the umbrella in the basement during a fugitive bright period at closing time.

Gran was drinking sherry in the kitchen while Mum washed salad at the sink, presumably keeping an eye on her intake.

"Can I have one?" Dora seized the bottle before Mum could refuse. Instead she frowned, only half playful.

"I don't know ... the boozing gene skipped a generation with me."

"What about your Martinis? Anyway, I don't booze, I just feel happy. Isn't that the best time to drink?"

"Certainly more sensible than flying to the bottle for consolation when you're miserable," Gran said, and slyly raised her glass in Dora's direction, meanwhile nodding towards Mum. She had had her word.

Dora sat and watched them bickering companionably while the rain rattled on the window panes, shaking the green leaves in the garden, and almost longed for winter, the three of them shut in warmly against the world.

"What are you smiling about?" Mum said.

"I've had such a nice day. I do like the shop."

"I've been looking out some books for you to take in on Monday," Gran said. "Good stuff, too, none of your Victorian three volume novels and bound sets of Punch."

"Of course not," Dora said. Gran's books were all upstairs in her rooms, in glass-fronted bookcases, and in beautiful condition.

"No first editions," Gran said, "but they might fetch a pound or two for the cause."

"They aren't suffragettes, Mother," Mum said.

"Well, all good works are a cause, aren't they?" Gran said, expansively. "Just another drop, darling, while you've got the bottle."

"Sorry, Gran, there isn't another drop."

"You're joking." Mum's head jerked round.

"No." Dora upended the bottle and shook it. "Don't look at me. I've only got about half an inch here."

"Don't worry," Gran soothed them. "I've got plenty upstairs."

Mum had turned back to the sink, shoulders slumping. "I'm sure you have."

Dora was half-way down the steps on Monday before Gran overtook her.

"Can't wait to get there, can you?" Gran complained.

"No," Dora said, frankly. In her mind she was already striding down Lower Dukes Lane.

"What about the books?"

"Books?"

With a beautifully assumed look of mute reproach, Gran held out a dark green carrier bag.

"Harrods! When do you ever go to Harrods?"

"When I'm passing," Gran said, loftily.

"I bet you only went once and kept the bag to flash around. Maggie, at school, bought a blouse in a jumble sale with a Harrods label, and when it got too small she cut off the label and sewed it into a coat from C&A."

"Vulgar ostentation."

"And this isn't?" Dora looked inside and saw seven pristine dust jackets. "Gran! These are new."

"Not at all. Just *cared for*. You know I can't bear to see lovely things mistreated."

"You'd better not come to the shop, then. We've got some horrid old tomes in the basement. I suppose you want the bag back?"

"Well . . . it's a perfectly good bag."

"You *do* flash it around, don't you? All right, I'll bring it back tonight."

At the corner she turned and looked back. Gran was standing on the steps, posed like a svelte model in a magazine, framed by the tendrils of wisteria that grew over the porch. This year's fashions for the *Older Woman*, Dora thought. What an old ham she is; and walked on, her mind half in the shop, half back at the house with Gran and Mum, except that Mum was out at work. How had elegant posy Gran produced blunt, dour, downright Mum? And how had Mum in turn produced extravagant John, and Dora who knew so well how to be happy? Obviously Dad and Grandpa had contributed something. Grandpa had been a chartered accountant, not the most fanciful of professions, and Dad's capacity for being happy had removed him from the scene six months after Dora's birth, in search of fresh wife and children new.

She entered the shop with confidence, the Fresh-Water badge in place on her lapel, and went straight to the basement. Lou was telephoning and waved as Dora reached the foot of the stairs.

"New books," Dora mouthed, holding up the Harrods bag.

Lou, who probably supposed that a passing donor had given them to her on the way in, smiled in the distracted manner of people on the telephone who can never quite shake off the conviction that the party on the other end of the line can see them, and pointed towards the hole in the wall where Tony did his sorting and pricing.

Tony was currently manning the cash register. Dora had no idea what kind of a system he operated, for the boxes of books seemed to have been opened at random, in no particular order, but near the entrance was an avalanching heap of carrier bags awaiting their turn. She would have deposited Gran's contribution on top of the pile, but if it indulged Gran's harmless vanity to bring back the Harrods bag, it would be no harm to take out the books and leave them in a more prominent position on one of the boxes. In any case, she thought, looking at the mould-spotted volumes in the box through which Tony was apparently working, it would surely lift his heart to see Gran's gifts, shining cleanly in the murk. She folded the bag, shoved it in her pocket, hung her jacket next to Lou's raincoat and sprinted up the stairs.

"You'll never guess what I've just sold," Tony said, as she relieved him at the till. "Remember that frightful anatomy book I showed you on Saturday?"

"The one with a spider living in the spine?"

"That one. A South African tourist came in a little while ago and *grabbed* it. Said his grandfather owned one and he used to spend hours looking at the pictures when he was a little boy. What sort of a boyhood was that? I asked myself. I thought it would be a cert for the pulping box," Tony said. "Are you taking over?"

"Yes please."

"You *like* being on the till? Don't you get bored?"

"That's what Lou said. No, I do like it. I enjoy watching people."

She changed places with Tony and watched him, descending from the sunlit shop to the dismal regions below. Tony, she had learned from Lou, was a teacher, generously giving up his holiday to help out, as well as coming regularly on Saturdays. Why didn't they have teachers like him at her school? instead of the glum functional types who seemed to regard the students as some kind of industrial raw material, rather than people, and often asked her irritably what she had to be so cheerful about.

Tony was at work around the corner when it was Dora's turn to go down for coffee, but as she was boiling the kettle she heard his voice:

"Good Lord, this is one of ours."

"What is?" Lou said.

"Balcon's *Flora of Northern Europe*. I thought I recognized it."

"I suppose someone's decided not to keep it after all." Lou sounded preoccupied.

"I remember putting it on display. Look, here we are, on the fly-leaf – June. That must have been the first week I was pricing, at half term. That's my writing."

"Maybe it was an unwanted present."

"Well, whoever bought it only had it for six weeks. It could take six months to get through this thing. How odd."

Dora stirred her coffee. She was fairly sure that the *Flora of Northern Europe* was one of the books in Gran's carrier bag. Holding the mug gingerly for fear of spilling hot liquid on delicate volumes, she sidled out of the kitchen cupboard and peered round the

88

corner. Tony and Lou were standing with their backs to her but she could see that Tony had already begun pricing the books from the Harrods bag. One lay open with his yellow pencil laid across it.

"How much did it go for last time?"

"Ten pounds, it was in perfect nick. It still is. I'll just change the date and put it out again – for the same price. It doesn't look as if it's been opened."

"There's a gap in the window display," Lou said. "Dora! Oh – there you are. When you go up again just check the window display, will you? I noticed some wide open spaces."

"You can put this in for a start," Tony said. He leaned across the boxes and handed Dora the *Flora*. "It's a bargain, though no doubt someone will try to haggle over it."

Dora took it as Tony bent again over his open book and picked up his pencil, murmuring, "I don't suppose this one . . . no, Dillons."

Dora sat on the stool that held open the kitchen door and balanced the *Flora* on her knee while she leafed through it. Definitely it was one of Gran's. As soon as she saw the spine she recognized it from the glass fronted bookcase in Gran's sitting room, the one between the two long windows. She felt vaguely uneasy; the feeling had first stirred back there in the pricing room when Tony said, "Whoever bought it only had it for six weeks." If Gran had bought it only six weeks ago she would surely have remembered something, said something like, "Oh, that's where I bought Balcon's *Flora of Northern Europe*." Or, when she gave Dora the Harrods bag this morning, something like, "This one's going back where it came from. Can't think why I bought it," or something, *something.*

When Dora saw Lou and Tony looking at it she had been about to say, "My grandmother sent those"; now

89

she shivered with relief that she had held her tongue, had taken the books out of the Harrods bag that she had so blithely waved at Lou when she arrived, for now she had herself remembered something. When she first came home and told Gran about the shop, Gran had not known where it was. She recalled that distinctly. Gran had known the *place*, all right, but she had thought it was still a restaurant.

Dora rinsed out the coffee mug and went to look on the stock shelves for books to take upstairs. Everything was labelled: Psychology, Engineering, Pets, Fiction, Medicine – some of the medical books were so old they were dangerous; one advocated igniting gunpowder to cauterize dog bites, and the shelf which carried the most inviting looking items was labelled simply, Display. These were the books that could be stood on top of the shelves upstairs, laid on the table by the door or exhibited in the window. It did not seem to matter what they were about, they were in sufficiently good condition to command a decent price. Making a tray of an atlas, she loaded it with a dozen or more and set off upstairs. As she went she heard Tony's voice; "Well I'm damned, here's another; July."

She did not wait for the rest.

Mum was in the little back garden, tenderly drawing tap-rooted weeds out of the borders. Dora stood watching her for a few minutes, marvelling at her patience. Dora always tugged too hard and left half of the root behind to sprout again. Gran never weeded at all, but floated about with a trug over her arm, snipping off dead heads with the languorous motions of a dying ballerina. Only Mum really enjoyed gardening, the continuous day to day dedication to flowers and weeds alike; planting, pruning, mowing, mulching, digging. She was humming under her breath, something enjoyably mournful in a minor key. She never did that in the house.

I never want to leave here, Dora thought. I'd like us to go on for ever, Mum in the garden, Gran upstairs and me coming home from work. I want to be me coming home from work *always*.

"Mum?"

"I thought I heard you come in. Had a good day?"

Mum, I do love you even if you are an old crab and won't let Gran have her gin. "Of course I did."

"Remember to get the eggs?"

"They were out of free range. I'll go down to Assad's later, if you like. Where's Gran?"

"Having an *aperitif*, I expect." Mum's voice dulled again. "Don't leave it too late, will you?"

"He's open till ten."

"You know I like us to eat by eight."

"I'll go in a minute," Dora said, turning back to the house. Why did they have to eat by eight – in case Gran had too many *aperitifs*?

Gran was standing on the balcony with a long-stemmed glass in her hand.

"Flirting with the rain," Gran said.

"Is it raining?"

"A few drops. I'm daring it to do its worst." She trilled her fingers along the wisteria fronds. "Do you want some Rudesheimer?"

"I'll wait till dinner. Mum's doing a soufflé, only I've got to go out again for the eggs."

"Don't rain on my Dora," said Gran to the sky.

"Gran, where did those books come from?"

"Books?"

"The ones you gave me for the shop – oh, here's your precious bag. Gran, they were almost new."

"Then they should fetch a good price."

"They will." Ten pounds for Balcon's *Flora*. "But

91

didn't you want them? You can't have had them long." June. July.

"Good heavens, darling, I buy on impulse, you know me. Sometimes I make the most ghastly mistakes, that appalling linen dress for instance. I've never worn it. I'm even worse when it comes to books. 'I *must* have that,' I think. 'Just the thing for long winter evenings,' but," she shrugged sweetly, "when the long winter evenings come, I've utterly lost interest."

"You really should come along to FreshWater," Dora said, blushing. "It's a much cheaper way of buying on impulse. We've got some lovely bargains."

"I dare say I shall, darling. Where did you say it was?"

"Just us today," Lou said on Wednesday. "Jo's rung in to say she's got some kind of bug. Tony's had to take his son to an athletics meeting, though I should think they'd be rained off at this rate."

"Till or shelving?" Dora said briskly. Susan was already half-way up Lower Dukes Lane, her umbrella tugging wilfully in the wind.

"If you're happy at the till . . ." Lou said, smiling, as if she could scarcely believe it, and rushed to the basement where the phone was ringing.

The shop was empty. Dora sat at the cash register and craned her neck to inspect the window display. There were four books at least which looked brand new. She had identified Balcon's *Flora of Northern Europe*, in its central position, from the top of the lane.

Outside, the rain fell steadily; a mill race gurgled in the gutter that ran down the centre of the pavement. Up and down, with dogged tread and resigned expression, trudged inadequately clad tourists, and bareheaded macho blokes in sodden T-shirts who didn't care, trekking between the building site at the bottom and the Duke's Head at the top, but when the downpour eased and the sky lightened, people once more paused to look in at the window, and after a while began to venture inside.

Lou ran up and down with fresh stock for the shelves. A German in a plastic mac bought the *Flora* and Lou instantly darted in with a replacement, the complete works of Jane Austen. On the same trip she deposited, on the trolley near the door, a big glossy coffee-table book, *An Illustrated History of the English Theatre*. It was so large that Dora, seated at the till, could see the jacket design quite clearly. Predictably, a painting of The Globe with, especially predictably, Shakespeare standing on the stage, as if Shakespeare were the only person in England who had ever written a play.

It was while she was staring at the book that she noticed activity in the convex mirror that hung at the back of the shop. It took a moment to work out which set of shelves it reflected; the Natural History section, out of her line of sight, behind the stair well, but she recognized the figure at once, even though it seemed no larger than Shakespeare at The Globe. What she did not recognize was the grey macintosh cape. Dora leaned down and opened the door beneath the desk. It stuck a little and she had to jerk it, evidently it normally responded only to the drawer of the cash register. Squinnying sideways and attempting to watch the mirror at the same time, she read the second notice from the top, that was taped inside the cupboard door.

Elderly woman, tall, well dressed. Wears a grey cape. Never buys anything.

Dora saved time and motion by serving a customer before bothering to close the door; now trying to divide her attention between his Anglo-French queries about street maps, and the figure in the mirror which was, in fact, no longer in the mirror but proceeding round towards the Fiction corner, magisterial in its exquisitely tailored cloak of dove grey cloth, a little spotted with rain about the shoulders.

Dora shut the drawer and the door. The Frenchman left with a cheery wave. The grey cloak was moving towards the display table where it paused. Scrutinized, head bent. Straightened up and shrugged regretfully; no, nothing, absolutely nothing, nothing at all. And left.

Dora saw at once that Shakespeare had left as well and spun round to look out of the window where the grey cloak was unhurriedly adjusting itself, as well it might, to conceal what lay beneath. Dora broke her rule about catching the eye of passers-by – this was hardly a passerby – and looked, and looked.

Gran looked back, smiled and nodded and walked away down Lower Dukes Lane in the cloak that Dora had not known she owned. It was a friendly look, candid, impersonal, and held not a hint of guilt, or duplicity, or recognition.

The Gnomon

Handsome Daniel Maddison strolled through the hall of the Golden Wheel Guest House and chanced on a mirror that hung near the reception desk.

"Dan loves mirrors," his sister Clare had once said. "He can look at them for hours." He permitted himself a sidelong glance in passing, but halted when he heard his mother chatting in the coffee lounge with Mrs Glover, the proprietor. They were apparently discussing Daniel.

"Honestly," said Mrs Maddison, "you'd never think he was nearly sixteen."

Daniel and his reflection nodded to each other in tacit agreement. They could easily pass for eighteen, and often did.

"Sometimes he behaves like a five-year-old." Daniel scowled and moved closer to the door of the coffee lounge, the better to hear Mrs Glover's reply. Mrs Glover, schooled by years of discreet hospitality, spoke always with restraint, but it was Mrs Newcombe, a fellow guest, who answered his mother. Mrs Newcombe communicated through a built-in loud hailer.

"I'd never have suggested it, if I'd thought he'd mind," Mrs Newcombe yelled, elegantly.

"Just one afternoon he's been asked to give up, out of his entire holiday, and he's been sulking since breakfast," said Mrs Maddison. "Still, he's not going to upset poor Susie; I'll see to that."

Daniel's afternoon, which had been scheduled to include a naughty film at the ABC in town on the strength of his easily passing for eighteen, was to be sacrificed in the interests of lolloping Susie Newcombe from Leighton Buzzard who wanted to explore certain atmospheric ruins, a squalid pile of hard core on a nearby hillside, dignified as an ancient monument solely by the presence of a plaque erected by the Department of the Environment. Daniel's services as escort and guide had been rashly offered, and lacking his permission, by his mother who, without sharing it, liked to boast about his knowledge of archaeology. Both the Maddisons and the Newcombes had arrived at the Golden Wheel on the same day, but by adroit programming Daniel had avoided meeting Susie after the first confrontation at dinner on the evening of their arrival. This unfortunate introduction during which, after a day spent travelling, neither of the parties was at their best, had sealed Susie's fate as far as Daniel was concerned.

"I love old places like this," Susie had said, gesturing at the low ceilings and murky nooks of the Golden Wheel's dining-room. "I think this place is really spooky, don't you? Don't you?" Daniel remained silent and savaged his rhubarb crumble. "Don't you think it's spooky?"

"Not particularly," Daniel said. He detested words like spooky, eerie, spine-chilling; also weird, incorrectly used. "Just decrepit," he said flatly.

"But doesn't it make you *feel* weird?" Susie persisted. "I felt something, the moment I came in."

"I bet you did," Daniel mouthed, under the pretence of chewing rhubarb crumble.

"They've got a ghost," Clare chipped in. "I asked."

"I know. It's really weird how you can tell, isn't it?" Susie said. "Mrs Glover said it was a girl who crept out one day to meet her lover and he never turned up. Mrs Glover said she's still waiting."

"Has she seen her?"

"Nobody's seen her," Susie breathed. Crumbs flow. "Apparently you just sort of feel her, sort of waiting."

"*Weird.*"

"And you can smell roses. She was carrying roses."

"Has Mrs Glover ever smelled roses?"

"Yes. You can sometimes smell them even in winter. She said, if you ever smell roses, you'll know Maud's about – that was her name, this ghost; Maud Ibbotson."

"You'd have a job not to smell roses at this time of year," Daniel observed, looking out of the window at the July sun, low in the sky and flooding with rich colour the rose garden that lay beyond the windows.

"If I smell roses I shall *faint*," Susie remarked, allowing the skin in the jug of custard to flop like a flexible frisbee over her second helping of rhubarb crumble.

"It's really eerie, isn't it?" Clare said. "A ghost you can only smell. What happened to her, this Maud? Did she die of a broken heart, or something?"

"Oh no, I asked Mrs Glover. She said there was an accident. She had a fall, or something, while she was waiting, and when they found her it was too late to do anything, and she died."

"A fall? Out of a window?"

"I expect so. She'd be leaning out to look for him, wouldn't she? I wonder which one it was?" Susie looked round speculatively at the dining-room windows, and sniffed.

"I bet if we found it we should be able to feel something," Clare said.

Susie shuddered pleasurably. "Let's try. I've never seen a ghost, but I often *feel* things."

It was in order to commune with the past that

Susie wished to explore the ruins that afternoon, in Daniel's company. Susie would feel less weird in Daniel's company, according to Daniel's mother. "I thought feeling weird was the object of the exercise," said Daniel, but to no avail. He put his head round the door of the coffee lounge and flashed a hideous smile across his face, like a neon advertisement in Piccadilly Circus.

"Where are you off to?" Mrs Maddison asked, with base suspicion.

"To wait for Susie," Daniel said, affronted. Did she really think he was such a fool as to sneak off to the cinema? "I'll be in the rose garden – will you tell her when she comes down?"

He was not lying. He fully intended to wait for Susie in the rose garden but, so far as he knew, neither Susie nor his mother was aware that at the Golden Wheel there were two rose gardens; the one at the back, beyond the dining-room, and the other one. Daniel was going to wait in the other one.

He had discovered the second garden by accident while evading, as it happened, an earlier encounter with spooky Susie and her chilly spine. The official rose garden was broad and spacious with standard trees in circular beds, a blanched statue or two, and little white iron tables and chairs disposed here and there on the clipped turf. It reminded him of a crematorium. Along one side was a low rockery hedged with conifers that had had their tops nipped off in adolescence. Resolutely squaring their shoulders they now formed an impenetrable windbreak.

"They're pleached," said Mrs Newcombe, and with her daughter's vampire ability to fasten onto a harmless word and bleed it white, she repeated it at intervals, liking the sound of it. "Pleached." It described her voice very accurately, Daniel thought. He could hear her pleaching now as he slipped away from the house, crossed the lawn beyond the dining-room windows, and sidled between the cypress boughs of the conifer hedge, into the other rose garden.

He guessed that before the conifers were planted and the rockery raised, it had been an extension of the main garden, but now the windbreak obscured it entirely. Daniel, who had originally squeezed between the trees in an effort at hasty concealment, had been amazed to find himself in an open space instead of being, as he had expected, compressed between the conifers and a wall. Today he muttered, "Open, sesame," and passed straight through to stand at the head of the second rose garden. Unlike the public part, it seemed to exist for the sole purpose of growing roses. It was narrow. Heavy banks of pink blossoms, one could scarcely call them mere flowers, overhung a trellis on either side, and shaded lush grass that had been cut, but not recently. Yellow ramblers rambled; cream climbers rioted. At the far end was a wooden rustic seat, weathered to the shade of old pewter, and at the nearer, close to where he stood, was the only other furniture, a sundial. Daniel had expected to find an inscription on its bronze plate, *Tempus fugit* perhaps, and there was one, but not *Tempus fugit. Time and the hour run through the roughest day*, it said in Roman letters that encircled the Roman numerals. Daniel, recognizing the quotation, took it to mean that everything must come to an end if you wait long enough. The gnomon pointed at his back as he walked down the garden to the rustic seat.

"Come into the garden, Maud," said Daniel, the scent of roses clogging his flared nostrils, and suddenly suspected that it was here, and not in the

99

house, that Miss Ibbotson had come to her tryst. He waited for the sensation that ought to chill his spine as it certainly would have chilled Susie's. If Susie were there, would Maud Ibbotson manifest herself as she waited for her faithless lover who was now, according to Clare's researches, one hundred and twelve years overdue? He imagined her standing by the rustic seat, tall, stately, leaning several degrees from the perpendicular and counterbalanced by a bustle, like an old joke in *Punch*. She would be no joke if he did see her, but no one had ever seen her. They only smelled roses.

Daniel sat down on the rustic seat, propped his feet on the farther arm and settled back to read and yawn. Distantly, mercifully diminished by distance, Mrs Newcombe pleached on. From time to time the telephone rang in the reception hall, but in the rose garden, regardless of the sundial's admonition, time hung suspended. The roses, ripe for disintegration, nevertheless remained whole. Not a petal fell to the ground. Beyond the hedge a strident shriek, fit to chill the hardiest spine, split the gentle air.

"Danie-elll!"

He looked down discouragingly at his book.

"Danie-elll!" The voice advanced, receded, advanced again. Daniel, rather than look at the hedge in case Susie felt his penetrating gaze and discovered him, fastened his eyes upon the nearest rose, a swollen globe of lingerie pink, like something off a chorus girl's garter. He stared at it.

"Danie-el!"

Over-examined, the rose blurred and softened before his eyes, but when he refocused it was still there, and the voice, a little subdued, receded disconsolately towards the house. "Danny?" Daniel's left forefinger reached out and tipped the rose under the chin, but even now, on the point of dissolution, it remained on its stem.

"Daniel?" It was his mother's voice, sharpened by anger to Mrs Newcombe's pitch, and like a harpy echo Mrs Newcombe joined in. "Daniel?"

"I'm not here, dear," Daniel murmured. He heard their conversation in angular duet, his mother embarrassed and apologetic, Mrs Newcombe making light of things, but maternal, affronted on Susie's behalf. She and Mrs Maddison were already on Pat and Shirley terms.

"Oh Shirley, I'm *so* sorry. I can't think . . ."

"It's not *your* fault, Pat."

The telephone rang again. Daniel glanced up and saw the rose's soft sphere glowing at the very edge of his eyesight. When he reached the end of the chapter he would allow himself the pleasure of beheading that foolish, nodding flower, if it did not fall before he was ready for it.

Mrs Newcombe pleached unexpectedly close to the conifer hedge. Daniel's eyes were drawn unwillingly towards it, twin lasers drilling into the back of her crimped head through the dense branches (Go away, you old bat. Hop off.) and saw, near the sundial, a rose explode silently in a shower of pink petals. Daniel stared and absorbed what he had seen. It appeared that the rose had not so much dropped as *burst*. A little closer, the same thing happened again; a second rose vanished and this time the petals did not fall down, but flew up, as if a hand had clouted the rose from below. Daniel closed his own itching forefinger against his palm and saw a third rose evaporate. At the same time he felt his trouser leg stir against his shin, a web of hair unravel across his forehead. Waiting for his own rose to drop, as it surely must now that the wind had found its way into the garden, Daniel swung his feet to the ground and felt a current of air round his ankles, too low to fell a rose; and then, on the far side of the garden, a fourth blossom erupted with such violence that the petals were knocked into the foliage and lodged there. Not one reached the grass. Three blooms in close conference on one stem were struck apart. Daniel watched the drifting confetti and pondered upon the word *struck*. It was almost, Daniel thought, as if someone were walking round the garden and striking at the roses as he went: as she went: there . . . there . . . and *there*: someone who was waiting, and had tired of waiting, tired of roses. Now a dozen died together under a downward blow that dashed them to pieces, while a lateral swipe at another spray sent petals flying against Daniel's face, three metres distant.

Now she is using both hands, Daniel thought. Left and right – oh, our patience is *exhausted*, isn't it?

There was no wind in the adjacent garden where, over the tops of the conifers, Daniel could see a crack willow weeping its burden to the ground. Just beside him, fragments of his own rose took to the air and he heard the soft thud as it broke up. It was fearfully close.

Here she comes, said Daniel, not noticing that he had closed his book and now sat on the very edge of the rustic seat, one arm flexed against the silky wood to thrust himself upright. Here she comes. Not yet impelled to run, she strode, skirt sweeping the turf, beside one trellis, across to the other, across, along, and as she went her arm swung up and *there*, another rose gone, and another, and a whole blasted bouquet, there, there, and *there*.

Daniel drew in his feet as the imperious air swept by him. She was moving faster now, there, there, and *here*. Not a rose escaped that was ripe, and now she was laying into the half-blown flowers, tearing them alive from the branches, not pausing to crush them but flinging them behind her, grabbing at the next while the last was still airborn, arcing and diving. The grass was dappled all over, not only below the trellises, with pink and cream and yellow bruises. She tore at the very stems, twisting and ripping them from the briars. They were not thornless roses. Her hands were surely shredded, blood running down her scything arms to the elbow. And flayed to the bone as she must be, still she flung from one side to the other, wrenching and rending until even the buds were broken and hung down, dead before they were alive, as she cast herself from side to side, there, there, and *there.*

And then she stopped, wrecked, and let her bleeding arms dangle. Daniel, straining to see the thing he must avoid, lifted himself from the seat and began to edge across the grass towards the shelter of the trellis, eyes everywhere to see where the next rose would fall. But there was no next rose. In all the garden there was not one bloom intact, no living thing left to destroy.

Except me, said Daniel, and the air struck him in the face and spun him round so that he fell back against the seat and slithered to the ground, his head aching from side to side as though it were an arm that had felled him. He saw the grass creep and gleam, under pressure, as the tempest wrapped him round, in awful, forceful silence, and dragged him to his feet.

"No!" Daniel shouted. "Not me, not me. I never kept you waiting." He wrestled with the wind that surged and sucked at him until he began to stumble down the garden towards the sundial, with cold arms about his neck, cold skirts flapping about his legs, and a frozen face against his cheek. He thought she must throw him out of her garden, neck and crop, to punish him for keeping a poor girl waiting. But he soon saw that although he and she were headed for the conifers, before them, directly in his path, stood the sundial.

"No!" he shouted again, and leaned back against the wind that all at once gathered behind him and pushed, with horrible confidence, so that the slippery soles of his shoes skated over the grass and petals towards the stone column, the bronze dial, the shining gnomon. "No," he said, "no!" But a colder breath than his stopped the cry in his mouth, and a final thrust sent him reeling, headlong. His foot came down heavily on the greasy roses, turning his ankle, and he fell flat, on the grass, and at the same time heard a hissing whistle of breath that choked and stopped, bubbled, and died away. He lay at the foot of the sundial, one hand to his forehead where he had gashed it against the plinth, and looking up saw the gnomon pierce the cloudless sky, just where his heart would have been had his skid not thrown him to one side. It glistened wetly in the dry, still air.

After a long time he raised himself from the turf and crawled away through the conifers to the garden of the Golden Wheel, where his mother and Mrs Newcombe were spreading crockery and cakes on a little white iron table. They both turned round simultaneously and converged with shrill cries, hauling him upright.

"Whcro've you *heen*?" his mother demanded. Daniel pointed vaguely.

"In there."

"In where?"

"There."

"What are you talking about? Oh look, Shirley, his head. Daniel, what have you done?"

"The rose garden," Daniel said. "Don't go in the rose garden."

"This is the rose garden. What is he talking about?"

"Wandering," said Mrs Newcombe, wisely, mouth pursed. "You ought to get him inside to lie down, Pat. Can't be too careful with knocks on the head, especially just there."

Mrs Glover came towards them across the starry grass.

"An accident? Oh my, what's all this?" She took Daniel by the chin and examined his forehead. "That's a nasty one. Where did you get that?"

"In the rose garden, he says. I can't imagine what happened," Mrs Maddison was saying. "We just looked round and saw him lying over there, by the rockery. I can't get any sense out of him. He just keeps saying he was in the rose garden, but he wasn't, of course. *We* were. I can't think how he got there without anyone seeing him, and I can't get him to say what hit him. It looks like something sharp – right-angled, almost. Like the corner of something."

"Not this rose garden . . . that one." He tried to raise an arm to show them, but they bore him indoors and made him lie down on the cretonne covered settee in the coffee lounge.

"*I* thought he came out through the conifer hedge," said Mrs Newcombe.

"Oh." Mrs Glover looked so dismayed that the twittering conference fell silent. "Oh dear, *that* rose garden. Oh no, he shouldn't have gone in there."

"You mean there *is* another?" Mrs Maddison rounded on Daniel. "I suppose you were trespassing."

"Not trespassing." Mrs Glover hurried to intervene. "But we don't use it any more. It gets so windy." She looked at him. "Is that what happened, dear? It got windy?"

He nodded. Mrs Newcombe swooped over him with an icy dripping flannel and swabbed his forehead.

"Oh, nonsense. There hasn't been a breath of wind

all day," Mrs Maddison cried, vexed and put out. She hated scenes, especially scenes of Daniel's engineering.

"It's a funny place, that little garden," Mrs Glover said. "That's why we hedged it off. It seems to act as a kind of funnel. You get quite strong winds in there, even when it's still everywhere else." She laughed, almost apologetically. "Our little tempests, we call them."

Daniel thought of the wreckage that this little tempest had left behind it. He opened one eye and saw Mrs Glover looking at him. She telegraphed to him: *I know what you were doing in there, young man, and serve you right.*

He answered: *It's happened before, hasn't it? You ought to put up a wall.*

Mrs Newcombe was pleaching again. "He looked as if he'd seen a ghost."

"I didn't see anything," Daniel said, weakly. They came over to him and leaned down, all concern.

"Can you remember what happened, yet?" Mrs Maddison asked. "Did you have a fall?"

Yes, I had a fall, just like Maud. Maud had a fall, too. Do you know what she fell *on*?

"I was just reading," said Daniel, "and waiting for Susie."

"Susie was waiting for *you*," his mother retorted, asperity eroding sympathy.

"Where is she?"

"She went out with Clare, in the end. She got tired of waiting."

"She wasn't the only one," Daniel whispered, and turned his face to the cretonne back of the settee, to escape the slight smile that curled Mrs Glover's prim lips. In the end they gave up grilling him and left him to his own devices.

"A little sleep won't do any harm," said Mrs Newcombe.

When they had gone, back to their tea at the white iron table, Daniel sat up gingerly, and looked through the window towards the conifer hedge, behind which, among the scent of roses, Maud Ibbotson was still waiting, so angry, so desperate for company, her patience worn so dangerously thin.

Resurgam

From a dell of ferns and mosses the stony track led upward among the rocks, overhung here and there with green budding willow branches, past the cavernous mouth of the open tomb. The hillside was starred with little flowers; primroses, violets, squills, even daisies and early speedwell; tiny beads of moisture freckling the petals. But always you looked upward, over the balding rocks to the barren summit where the three crosses stood, stark, sinister, although unoccupied.

"And what's this?" The slender throat of Rowena Randall's brass plant-mister released a jet of vapour among the fronds around the tomb.

"Selaginella – club moss," Gilly Morton said. "Charlotte, do you have to grovel just there? It does rather give an impression of abject devotion."

"Isn't that what it's for?" Charlotte Morton rose from where she had been crouched on knees and elbows, with her chin resting on her forearms which was as close to the ground as she dared to get in the presence of Mummy and the vicar's wife. Alone she would have laid down on her side, one eye at least on ground level. As she stood up, the perspective declined and the lush little Calvary became a pile of breeze blocks piled against the most westerly arch in the north aisle.

"Of course that's what it's for – within limits. You

look as if you ought to be on a prayer mat, facing Mecca."

"Most of the devotion went into making it, I suspect," Mrs Randall said. "It's been here a week and this is the third time I've had to water it. I'd have thought Millie would have been running in and out night and day to see that it was fed and watered."

"Oh well, Millie's a true artist," Mrs Morton said, tolerantly. "It's the *creation* that counts. Once she's finished something she loses interest and goes straight on to the next. It was the same at the Patronal Festival."

"It's awfully clever, though," Charlotte said. "I mean, when you think it's all done with breeze blocks and pâté bowls – and the way she's made the track wind upwards."

"The hairpin bends, you mean," Gilly Morton said. "She got a trifle over-enthusiastic there, I think. It looks like a lay-out for the Jerusalem Grand Prix. Now, are you coming back with me or would you rather walk?"

"I'll walk home," Charlotte said. "I just want to stay here for a bit and enjoy the flowers."

"Well, don't fall into a trance and get locked in," Rowena said. "Jeremy will be locking up at six."

Charlotte, gazing once more at the Easter garden, heard their heels gossip towards the door.

". . . thinking melancholy thoughts and composing poems about suicide . . ." That was Mummy who had evidently been spying through her desk again.

"Oh well, at that age . . ."

Rowena Randall was a bitch, even if she was the vicar's wife. The heavy door in the south porch closed behind them with a boom and a clatter as the latch dropped. Charlotte kept her eyes on Golgotha, an outcrop of flints balanced on top of the breeze blocks with the crosses anchored in grey Plasticine. Wasn't this the time for melancholy thoughts? these hours between grim Good Friday and the day of Resurrection? There was nothing in the Bible about what they did on that terrible Saturday after the Crucifixion; grieving, shattered, panic-stricken. Sure as hell, though, they hadn't been flower arranging.

Mummy and Mrs Randall had done the altar flowers, two stout brass bowls of rampant white lilies. Lesser members of the flower roster had been charged with the wrought iron stands by the chancel arch, and the odds and sods, as Daddy called them, had been let loose on the window sills where long troughs were vulgarly crammed with loud yellow daffodils and swags of ivy. Millie Gainsborough, architect of the Easter garden, had also been allowed a little fling at the foot of the pulpit, where she had indulged her mania for breeze blocks in a kind of terrace, bearing pots of bulbs. Charlotte, idling in the lane that morning, had seen her unloading the breeze blocks from the back of her Morris Traveller. Millie carried them one in each hand, against her shoulders, her striped poncho flying in the March wind. She looked like Moses, bearing the Ten Commandments on tablets of stone.

The wind had dropped since then. It was chilly in the church now that the sun was descending, but Charlotte knew that she would be stepping out into an unseasonably mild evening. She drew her cold hands up into the sleeves of her jacket and walked the length of the church, from west door to altar, passing from the fresh exuberant scent of the daffodils to the heavy clinging perfume of the lilies in their twin bowls. Tomorrow the silver cross would be released from its protective custody in the vestry safe and displayed between them, flanked by the massive gilt candlesticks that shared its confinement.

"Nothing's sacred, these days," Rowena Randall

complained, after a neighbouring church had been looted of its altar plate, which was why Jeremy would be along to lock up at six.

As she had foreseen, walking out of the chill church was like entering a warm room. Charlotte carefully closed the door behind her, as exhorted by the notice in the porch, in case wayward birds or bats flew in. The notice was tacked up alongside the electoral roll, the flower roster – mainly blank because of Lent – the Bishop's Easter Message and a square of white card ploughed over by Rowena's dashing italic which soared and swooped in exotic pot hooks that tangled themselves illegibly with the line beneath.

HELP!!!! Rowena had exclaimed, winsomely. *Our lovely churchyard is fearfully overgrown. Would any kind souls lend a hand at getting it into shape for Spring? Call me or the vicar on 249. R. R.*

Perhaps it was the proximity of the Bishop's message, but Charlotte envisaged Spring proceeding up the lane in cope and mitre to peer testily over the wall at the tangle of dead grass, ivy and blackberry vines which had rampaged through the churchyard unchecked since the death of Peter Seals, who had husbanded it for fifty years. Even Peter's grave, the most recent and still awaiting its headstone, was engulfed by ground elder and the frayed remains of kecksies and dock.

Somewhere in that wilderness was buried gold, the generous clumps of daffodils that had once gilded the churchyard at Easter. It had been Peter's pride and personal devotion to lay one daffodil on every grave, ancient and modern – and some were very ancient – at dawn on Easter morning, so that when the congregation arrived for Matins it might feel, as Jeremy Randall regularly insisted in his sermon, that every villager past and present had joined together to celebrate the Resurrection. Given that the present

111

population was somewhere around 800 and the congregation rarely more than fifty, it occurred to Charlotte every year that there were certainly more dead celebrants than live ones. This year, though, there would be no daffodils laid out and scarcely any standing daffodils visible, let alone the more discreet clusters of grape hyacinth, primrose and violet. Rowena's girlish plea had been in the porch for three weeks without so much as jogging the elbow of anyone's conscience. Decorating the church, building an Easter garden, were more acceptable services to the Lord than laying in with a scythe to level his acre.

Charlotte stomped on a tussock or two, clearing a patch around the daffodils that stood by the gate. At least they would make a showing. In previous years the whole churchyard would have been clipped in late autumn so that by now the fragrant vernal grass would be showing its little low flowers.

Charlotte sighed and stepped back from the daffodils, straightening up surreptitiously as she heard a car slowing down in the lane. It drew up by the lich gate and Charlotte recognized the vicarage Volvo. However, it was not the vicar who stepped out, but his son Michael. He looked surprised when he saw Charlotte rise from the herbage on the far side of the gate, but only, she supposed, because he had not been expecting to see anyone at all.

"Oh dear," he said, "are you waiting to talk to Daddy?"

Michael Randall was twenty, in his first year at Cambridge. Charlotte was faintly startled to hear him refer to his father as "Daddy"; it seemed to reduce him by several inches to the little boy in a blue St Thomas's School cap, that was her earliest memory of him.

"No," Charlotte said. "I've been helping Mummy with the flowers."

"Oh, good," Michael said. He advanced through the squealing gate, another memento of Peter who had oiled it regularly. "He got called out, so I've come to lock up instead. Have you all finished inside?"

"Yes. Mummy – and your mother – went a little while ago. I was just looking round. It's a bit of a mess, isn't it?"

"Poor old Peter. Who'd think six months could make such a difference?" Michael walked towards the porch. Charlotte walked with him as they seemed to be talking to each other. She supposed this must be what you might call a happy accident, their meeting by chance like this, and she recalled all those times when she had made a detour past the vicarage and he hadn't come out. "I'd better just look round inside," Michael said. "Daddy always does – in case there's someone lurking, I expect."

"I was the last one out," Charlotte said.

"I'd better look. Mummy may have left the light on in the vestry. The wiring's a bit dodgy."

"You wouldn't think a church could catch fire," Charlotte said, as they went back inside.

"What, all that stone?" The echoing interior was dark now. Michael depressed a switch by the door and a single lamp glowed sullenly in the nave. "But think of York Minster, how that burned." He loped up the aisle and into the north transept where the vestry stood. Charlotte waited by the door. She *had* been thinking of York Minster, but not of the stone, only wondering why it was that God allowed his churches to catch fire at all, and especially by striking one with lightning. It seemed so pointless, burning down your own house.

A closing door thudded in the shadows and Michael

113

returned. At the end of the aisle he paused by the Easter garden.

"Isn't it frightful?"

"*Isn't* it?" Charlotte agreed, pulling the plug on her enchantment.

"All those pretty flowers. Do you think Jesus was admiring the violets as he carried the cross up?"

"Do they have violets in Palestine?" Charlotte asked, cautiously. *Why* was it frightful?

"They probably do now. The Israelis seem to grow everything. But really, think of the name; Golgotha; Place of a Skull. If I were making an Easter garden I'd just use rocks – and a few cacti perhaps – and I'd make it look just like a skull, grinning, you know? Gaping eye sockets – the tomb would be one of them. And the only things I'd put on it would be those three crosses at the top and right at the foot, a little tree with a noose hanging from it."

"For Judas?"

"Exactly," Michael said. "I think we should remember him, too. That's what it's all about, after all; betrayal; sacrifice."

"And resurrection," Charlotte suggested, and tapped with her toe the inscription on the tombstone where they were standing, that was set into the floor of the aisle. It was one word only, in curly script: *Resurgam*.

"Well, perhaps on Easter morning I'd let them scatter a few flowers." He smiled. "But why does everything have to be so pretty?"

He switched off the lamp and they went out again into the twilight. Charlotte lingered in the archway of the porch while Michael turned the enormous key in the lock.

"Talking of scattering flowers," he said, "I suppose no one's going to take over from Peter and do the decent thing?"

114

"The daffodils?"

"I always thought that was rather a nice gesture. Bit pointless this year, though. No one would see them, the place is so overgrown."

"Does that matter – that no one sees?"

"Of course not." She heard, rather than saw, his approving smile. "I might even get up early tomorrow and do it myself. It would be a nice surprise for Daddy."

"I'll help." Charlotte was amazed at her presumption.

"Would you? Well, yes . . . why not? What time does the sun rise? Is there a communion? We wouldn't want to be seen. That would spoil the effect."

"Sun rise is at six o'clock – about." Charlotte felt illuminated by a joyous, conspiratorial glow. "And we had communion here last week. It'll be at Shapton tomorrow."

"Right, I'll see you here at six. I'll bring some shears or a scythe. We might be able to clear a patch or two. Now, shall I give you a lift home?"

"No thanks, I was going to walk, anyway." It was hard to say. She would have loved to ride down into the village with him, but why spoil what was to come with anything so prosaic? Better to part here at the lich gate where they would meet again in twelve hours, at sunrise on a March morning.

She often went for early walks. No one would remark on her absence even if this walk were a little earlier than was customary. The ground would be wet; she put on boots and jeans, regretfully. A frock would have been nicer, but impractical, and she shivered, imagining the discomfort of damp cotton clinging muddily round cold scratched ankles.

As she walked up the lane in the morning half light, which was never quite the same as an evening dusk, she saw that he was there before her, propping his bicycle against the churchyard wall, and at last admitted her secret fear that he might change his mind or forget to turn up.

"Well done," he said, approvingly, as they went under the lich gate. "Now, why don't you pick the daffodils while I do a spot of trimming. How many shall we need?"

"Peter told me last year; two hundred and three. Well, it will be two hundred and six now; Mrs Kellett and John Dawes, and Peter, since then."

"You'd think there'd be more."

"That's only the marked ones. There must be a few thousand down there, if you go right back to the beginning."

"In layers."

The churchyard, apparently a neat rectangle seen from the road, sprawled away downhill on the north side, ending in a ragged boundary of ditch and hawthorn hedge. It was here that the daffodils grew thickest, down behind the shed where the bier was kept along with the grindstone on which Peter Seals had sharpened his grave-digging spade. Some of the oldest graves lay on that side, scarcely more than humps in the rank grass. The light was still poor; clouds hung low and there was unlikely to be a sunrise. Charlotte stumbled between the graves, following what remained of the path that for half a century Peter had trodden to and from the shed, and countless sextons for countless years before him; back and forth, digging graves and filling them in, raising mounds, setting stones, unobtrusively clipping, cutting, planting, year in, year out. The practice of placing a daffodil on each grave had been long established when Michael's father became vicar; perhaps it was Peter himself who had begun it.

She could see the daffodils now, not a riotous yellow

116

in the sunless morning but glowing steadily, like shaded candles. She had cut an armful, and laid them in carefully counted bunches of ten, when a sound from the far side of the church made her stand erect and listen. Subconsciously she had been expecting to hear the clash of Michael's shears as he attacked the weeds and brambles on the south side. Now she realized that what she *had* heard was a car, and that what she was currently hearing was a conversation, conducted at a pitch that carried it over the roof of the church and down to where she stood, knee deep in daffodils.

Dropping the bunch that she held, uncounted, she began to run back through the long grass between the graves, to cut round the west end beneath the tower. There was something very familiar about one of those voices – the other, of course, was Michael's – and as she turned by the buttress she saw the roof of Millie Gainsborough's Morris Traveller above the coping of the wall; and there, harassing Michael over the lich gate, was Millie herself, armed not with a breeze block for once but a sickle. In her leather jerkin and shapeless felt hat she looked like the vanguard of a peasant mob come to strike the first blow against the clergy at the outbreak of revolution.

"Oh!" Millie squawked, when she noticed Charlotte. "I see."

Charlotte's disappointment almost took her voice away. "Have you come to do the daffodils?"

"Considering the state of the churchyard," Millie said, bitterly, "it did not occur to me that any one else could *conceivably* have thought of it. If Peter could see it now he'd be turning in his grave." She pushed open the gate and joined them. "Did you ask anyone's permission?"

"No," Charlotte said, and emboldened by Michael's presence added, "Did *you*?"

117

"I am on the flower roster," Millie said, implying that anyone who was not might consider herself lucky to get a mention on Judgement Day. "And as no one else on the roster seemed to have given a thought to keeping up Peter's life's work, let alone the daffodils – "

She was cut short by the sound of a motor horn, close at hand, and round the bend came Miss Jowett, also of the flower roster, but less of it, weaving up the middle of the road on a bicycle and defying the efforts to overtake of a car that was pursuing her, honking fretfully. Charlotte still further downcast, recognized the car at once, and the driver.

"Mummy!"

Mrs Morton braked and clambered from the driving seat, and Miss Jowett dismounted, still maintaining her position in the centre of the lane. The basket attached to Miss Jowett's handlebars contained shears, a billhook and a nasty-looking implement with teeth and an adjustable handle. Strapped to the roof rack of the Mortons' Peugeot was a scythe.

"Is this some kind of a conspiracy?" Mummy demanded coldly. "Good God, Charlotte, what are you doing here?"

"Michael and I thought it would be nice to put out the daffodils, as Peter couldn't do it any more," Charlotte mumbled.

"It might have been more sensible," Mrs Morton hissed, "to have consulted me first. I dare say it seemed very romantic to be frolicking at sunrise in the churchyard – "

"We wanted it to be a surprise," Michael said, gallantly, but Charlotte, miserable and embarrassed, observed that Mummy's spiteful barb had found its mark. *Romantic*. He was looking at his feet. Why were men always so frightened?

Miss Jowett had leaned her bike insultingly

against the nearside wing of the Peugeot and was toying with her implement. It made an unpleasant snickering noise as the teeth ground together.

"It does seem strange that everyone was being so secretive," Millie Gainsborough sniffed.

"Given the neglect that our churchyard has fallen into since last September, it hardly seemed worth consulting anyone else." Miss Jowett gnashed her surrogate fangs. "Obviously no one cared about maintaining standards."

"Actually," Michael said, with a nervous laugh that was very like his father's, "actually, it seems that quite a lot of people cared. I mean, now that we're all here . . ."

"It would still be a surprise," Charlotte said, "wouldn't it?"

"For whom?" Millie snapped.

"For everyone else."

"*Is* there anyone else?"

It struck Charlotte that in truth no one wanted to give anyone else a nice surprise. The whole thing had been an exercise in self-publicity: Lo! I alone remembered. Except for herself and Michael, of course. Michael really had wanted to please his father and she . . .? She *had* wanted to help, but was that for the vicar's sake, or for the sake of Peter's memory, or was it just for the chance of being alone with Michael at the break of Easter morning?

"You'd better get that thing out of the road," Millie Gainsborough said to Mummy. "I can hear a car coming."

"*Would* you move your machine?" Mummy simpered at Miss Jowett, as she climbed back into the Peugeot.

"I think that Mrs Gainsborough's taking up rather more of the verge than is strictly necessary or safe," Miss Jowett remarked, to no one in particular.

The car, which they could all hear now, came into view, slowed down and halted, confrontationally, nose to nose with the Peugeot, like two bellicose male beasts contending for the bony carcass of Miss Jowett's bicycle which was now trapped between them.

"Oh Jesus," Michael said, not at all prayerfully. The latest car was the vicarage Volvo, with Rowena at the wheel, her chin honed for the fray, and behind the car, towed in a trailer, a petrol mower, a rake and, inevitably, a scythe.

"Is something happening that I don't know about?" Rowena asked, glaring out at them through the passenger window.

"A happy accident," Michael said with a sickly smile, *exactly* like his father's. "We all had the same idea of coming up here early to tidy things a bit and put out the daffodils."

Rowena saw him for the first time.

"Oh!" she said. She pronounced it *eau*. "And what's your part in all this?"

For the second time the Cambridge undergraduate dwindled to a scrawny schoolboy.

"He was here first!" Charlotte cried, wounded with pity for him. "It was his idea!"

Rowena ignored her and continued to glare at her son who nibbled nervously at the air with his shears.

"I thought it would be a nice surprise for Daddy," Michael said.

"*Eau!*" Rowena said again. "And do you honestly suppose that chucking a few *flahrs* about is going to make up for the things you said to him last night, you bigoted little tit?"

"Well, why've *you* come?" Michael demanded. "*You* said that Peter was a sentimental old basket case with his *daffydils*." Michael was very nearly spitting with disgust. "You've said it every Easter for the last twelve years! You don't give a damn about the

120

churchyard. You just want to show everybody else up. Well, they beat you to it, didn't they?"

Rowena slammed the gears into reverse and the car shot backwards. The forgotten trailer jack-knifed on its towbar and there was much grinding and clashing as the lawn mower bucked in its chains, followed by an evil hissing as air escaped from a wrenched tyre on the trailer. The spectators, who had taken on the appearance of a well-armed garden party, converged on the Volvo to steady and restrain, while Rowena backed it on to the grassy clearing at the end of the churchyard wall.

Charlotte looked hopelessly at Michael. "I'm sorry."

"Bit of a fiasco, really," he said, not returning her look.

"They've ruined it!" Charlotte could have wept. "Why are people so hateful?"

Michael shrugged. "Six of us will get done faster than two. I should stay out of it if I were you. Get back to picking daffodils before those harpies beat you to it."

The flower roster was filing, barging, through the lich gate which screamed repeatedly as it swung since no one would hold it open for anyone else. When they were assembled on the path they all drew breath to take command.

"Right – " they said, simultaneously.

"Perhaps I could suggest – "

"If I might suggest – "

"May I make a suggestion – "

"If no one else has any suggestions – "

Michael turned wearily to them.

"I've already started," he said, "and I might as well go on here along the path. Mummy, why don't you cut around the graves with the mower? Mrs Morton, could you trim the verges? Miss Jowett, you and Mrs Gainsborough could start cutting back the brambles

– you've got the tools for it. At least we'll be able to see the daffodils when Charlotte's picked them."

Charlotte, on her way round the tower again, looked back. Like big sulky schoolgirls the four ladies fanned out to their allotted tasks, cowed by Michael's masculine authority. Since they had no intention of following each other's suggestions, they had no option but to act on his. Anyway, he was a man, even if his mother had just described him as a bigoted little tit, and he had called her a harpy. Charlotte turned and walked on. The sun was rising at last; the light was clean and cool and lay in streaks and splashes across the grassy graves. The daffodils sparkled by the hedge. On the hummock nearest to Charlotte's left foot, unmarked by kerb or stone, lay a long pale bone, underlined by a long dark shadow.

She stopped in mid-stride and looked again. In that arrested second she had had time to assume that what she was seeing was in fact a stick of peeled wood, gleaming in the new young sunlight; but no, it was definitely a bone, a clean white shin, placed accurately in the middle of the grave.

She had no urge to touch it. It did not look like the remains of a meal left by fox or dog; it was a human shin. Nor did it look as though it had worked its way out of the earth, exposed by wind and rain. Her eye travelled to the next grave which was almost entirely overgrown but had a flat slate tablet to mark its place. On the tablet stood a vertebra.

At the same moment someone at the east end of the churchyard screamed, the scream echoed by Millie Gainsborough's anserine quack, amplified by shock or disgust, and then a little chorus of shrieks and wails. Charlotte spun round and went back, running, seeing as she ran that all about her on the graves that had stood before in shadow and were now

122

illuminated, little patches of white winked cheerfully at her.

On the path by the lich gate the flower roster was gathered, collectively heaving with outrage. Michael stood placidly among them, holding a rib.

"Black Magic," Millie was gibbering; "sacrilege, blasphemy, filthy practices, desecration – "

Rowena clutched at Michael, his bigotry forgotten. "Thank God Jeremy hasn't seen this."

"But *when*?" Miss Jowett was bleating. "When? We were all here . . ."

Mummy turned to Charlotte. "You were the last to leave last night. Did you see anything?"

"What's happened?" Charlotte said, asking Michael, who was examining the rib with a donnish air and a squint.

"Can't you see?" Millie squealed, and gyrated, arms outflung, as if hooligans were realigning a signpost. "On the graves – all the graves – "

Charlotte looked, and on each grave – table tomb, headstone or simple mound – lay that same white token; some long, some minute, some curved, some rounded, all shining innocently to greet the morning.

"The police," Rowena said. "The police. Somebody call the police."

"We ought to move them."

"Not before the police have examined them. Evidence . . ."

"I said," Mummy broke in, "didn't you see anything, Charlotte?"

"It was getting dark when we left," Charlotte said. "The sun had set."

"We?" Rowena said, nastily.

"I was here when Michael came to lock up. That's when we decided to come back here this morning, and it was pretty dark then, too. I didn't see anything."

"This was done by night!" Miss Jowett declaimed.

"How could anyone do it in the dark?" Charlotte said. "There must be one on every grave; no one could have done it in the dark. Most people couldn't find the graves by daylight. Only Peter – "

"There are two hundred and six bones in the human body," Michael said. "Just enough to go round."

"Is that meant to be a joke?" Rowena asked him. "Have you got no feeling at all?"

Michael's eyes met Charlotte's at last. He said, "No, not a joke. This isn't a joke. Someone's got here ahead of us, that's all, only he wasn't in any condition to pick daffodils. Where is Peter buried, Charlotte? Have you looked at Peter's grave?"

Do You Read Me?

It was the custom to bring back yearly reports, signed, at the beginning of the autumn term, to prove that they had been shown to parents, or at least to a competent forger. Fenton, the Fifth Year tutor, was At Home in his office on Friday morning to receive them. When Rodney King clinked in with his report and laid it on the desk under Fenton's nose, Fenton looked at it, looked at Rodney, crossed his knees, folded his hands, and sat back with the air of a man who has prepared a little speech.

"It's a good one, in most respects, especially for Art and Design, I see. A+, eh? Parents pleased?"

Rodney nodded.

"Only there's this nasty little rider here, to the effect that you have difficulty in communicating. What does that mean, do you think?"

Rodney shrugged.

"It could mean that you don't say much for yourself. Might that be the trouble? A bit of a loner, are you? No close friends?"

Rodney made a non-committal noise through the slit between his front teeth.

"Your written work's excellent – no complaints from anyone about that – but you've got to learn to verbalize. You'll be doing GCSE English, this year. What's going to happen when you come to the oral?"

Rodney's hand described a gesture that dealt dismissively with the English oral. He took a step backward to indicate that he thought the interview might usefully be concluded.

"It's no good relying on badges to do your communicating for you," Fenton said. "I mean, it's very reassuring to see you covered in slogans for Nuclear Disarmament and Rock against Racism, but any idiot can pin on a badge. How many have you got?"

Rodney was moved to verbalize. "Seventy-three."

"And are you wearing them all?"

"Yes, Sir."

"Look, King, don't feel that I'm criticizing gratuitously, but when the Headmaster abolished school uniform for the Fifth and Sixth Forms, I doubt if he intended you to come to school in armour plate. You look like a pearly king under a microscope. The people who sit behind you don't do any work; they spend all their time reading your badges."

"I could move to the back," Rodney offered, helpfully.

"Don't think of it," Fenton said. "We might lose touch with you altogether. Just move the badges from the rear of that cut-price Biggles outfit – and the sleeves. Be selective, King. Use your designer's eye. Just a few, here and there, tastefully arranged, should be quite aesthetically pleasing. We'll get the message – *one* message at a time. OK?"

Rodney returned to school on Monday with his bomber jacket feeling several pounds lighter, and ran into Fenton in the corridor where he was pinning a sheet of foolscap to the Fifth Year notice board.

"Book Fair," said Fenton. "October 8th, St Stephen's Hall. Want to come? Sign here."

Rodney wove a deprecating pattern with his toes on the vinyl tiles, and the collar of his jacket rose about his ears.

"Oh, King, what eloquent shoulders you do have," Fenton said. "I'll take silence for consent. There, you can put your name down right at the top of the list. I suppose that elaborate routine is meant to suggest that you have nothing to write with? Tough titty," said Fenton, whipping out his biro, and writing Rodney's name in cock-eyed capitals at the head of the paper. "No one," Fenton observed, "would know that you hadn't written it yourself. And now I'll tell you something you'll really like. At this book fair they will have real live authors – and a badge-making machine."

The lower forms went down to the Book Fair in supervised groups. The Fifth Year, as befitted the enormous strides that they had made in self-discipline during the summer holidays, were left to find their own way. Rodney attached himself word-lessly to a sauntering cluster comprising the visual cream of his class: Eddie Hobson, known as Hobbers, and his three young ladies: Anna Miles, Katy Matthews, and Liz Salkey, the one with the eyes, the one with the ankles, the one was absolutely every-thing in between and all of it, by popular repute, promised to horrible Hobbers. Rodney suspected that they considered themselves too pretty to be seen associating with his own plain person, but knowing that if they told him to go away he would neither answer nor go away, they allowed him to slouch behind them to the hall.

Inside, they looked round in disdain.

"It's all kids' stuff," Katy said. "Little baby books and posters. Fenton's pulled a fast one on us."

"All this way and nothing to read," mourned Hob-bers, who had never yet been caught in possession of a book. "Can't even read old King these days, since Fenton debadged him. I bet you took the filthy ones off, King."

"He never had any filthy ones," Anna said.

"He did," said Hobbers, quietly, "Only he's so thick

127

he doesn't know they were filthy." Liz, lovely Liz, said nothing at all.

Rodney set off round the hall. There were five live authors, all looking repellently like teachers, several thousand books, a man flogging literary T-shirts, and the badge-making machine. The queue for badges stretched down one side of the hall, and Rodney attached himself to the tail of it, feeling like Gulliver in Lilliput among so many first school children, all squeaking like unoiled roller skates. Fenton had reminded everyone to bring money with which to buy books, to be signed by the live authors. Rodney had brought two pounds with which he bought ten badge blanks. The little kids all round him were scrawling their names in orange or turquoise, and drawing Dracula, with bats. Rodney brought his A+ for Art and Design into play. He heard Liz addressing Hobbers.

"Let's both get a badge made. I'll have your name and you have mine."

"Get out of it," said the gallant Hobbers. "I might get taken for King in a bad light."

"I'll make you a badge, Liz," Rodney said, suddenly, before he had time to lose courage. "What would you like?"

"You stick to scribbling on your own walls, beautiful," Hobbers said obscurely, with throaty threatening noises, and Liz was hauled away, badgeless.

Monday lunchtime brought Fenton and Rodney together again.

"I fear we're going to see a lot of each other this term," Fenton sighed. "You're sailing perilously close to the wind, King. You don't want a total embargo on your cargo, do you?"

Rodney had been practising a new gesture over the weekend. He raised his left eyebrow.

"ROD AGAINST RACISM I like," said Fenton. "ROD AGAINST THE BOMB is morally impeccable. However, NO FLIES ON ROD is another matter. When I told you to take the bloody things off your jacket, I didn't mean that you should put them anywhere else. That scrum at break, round the coffee machine, was largely caused by your reading public, King, on its hands and knees, perusing your jeans. What the hell is that on the back of your neck?" Rodney turned round so that Fenton could see the badge on his collar: KING'S HEAD. NO COACHES.

"Exquisite lettering. I said nothing on your back."

"It's under my hair, unless I look down," Rodney protested.

"It's under your *back* hair," Fenton said. "Edit yourself, King."

Rodney edited himself drastically, removing KING CAN SERIOUSLY DAMAGE YOUR HEALTH, NO U TURNS, NO S BENDS, NO Y FRONTS and DANGER, CONCEALED EXIT from their carefully chosen sites, leaving only a striking model in severe black type on white, after the fashion of London Transport: WATCH THIS SPACE, which he wore until Wednesday.

WATCH THIS SPACE provoked a gratifying curiosity among his readership. Even Hobbers and his little harem displayed some interest in his frontage. When public response had, he judged, reached its peak, he removed WATCH THIS SPACE and pinned another badge in its place.

"Oh look – a new one," Anna cried, homing in on it. A moment later she recoiled and walked back to Katy with an affronted expression.

"What does it say?" Katy asked. "Something disgusting?"

"Read it yourself, if you want to know," Anna said, sulkily. Katy stood up and approached Rodney's table. Rodney obligingly angled his shoulder the better to display his lapel. Katy leaned toward him, flushed, and backed off. Finally Liz, curious in spite of herself, wandered over.

"What does it say, Rod?"

"You wouldn't want to read it," Rodney said, and folded his arms over his chest. "I've got a different one for you." He was aware of Hobbers, glowering over by the window in an attitude of Neanderthal aggression. "You can look at it later on."

"Can't I see it now?"

"Not here." Rodney looked shocked. "See you at break – outside the library." He rose swiftly and went out.

"Well then," Hobbers demanded, with menaces, "what did it say? What's his badge of the week or flavour of the month this time, then?"

"I don't know. He wouldn't let me look," Liz said.

"You keep away from him and his badges," Hobbers said. "I don't know what the attraction is, the boring little git."

"He's funny," she said.

"Funny?"

"Anyway, attraction's not something you'd know much about, is it?" Liz said, shortly. She joined Katy and Anna on their way to class.

"Did you see what it said?" Katy asked.

"No. What did it say?"

"IF YOU CAN READ THIS YOU ARE TOO CLOSE," Anna snapped.

Liz smiled. "Oh."

"What are you grinning about?"

"I suppose that's why he wouldn't let me read it," Liz said.

At break she went to find Rodney outside the deserted library. He was there, his lapel vacant, and wearing a tie. On the knot of the tie was a badge.

"It better not be something foul," Liz warned him.

Rodney mimed affronted innocence. Would I do that? asked his arching eyebrows.

Liz leaned toward him and studied the legend: READ THE SMALL PRINT. "Is that all?"

"Of course it isn't. *Read* the small print."

"I can see that. What small print?"

"Round the edge," said Rodney.

"That?" Liz peered, inches away. "That squiggle? I thought it was the border."

"It's not a squiggle. It's small print: very small print."

"Get away, I can't read that."

"You can if you come near enough," Rodney said, and held his breath, praying that he had not taken the onions out of last night's hamburger in vain.

"Is it going to be worth it?"

"It's for *you*."

"And it's not something filthy?"

"Liz," Rodney said, solemnly, "if you don't trust me, you'll never find out what it says, will you?"

She was squinting past his chin now. "I still can't read it."

"You'll have to come closer, then, won't you?" and he closed his eyes, saying silently, Oh God, make it work, and when he opened them again she was still there, right under his nose, reading the world's smallest love letter round the edge of his tenth badge. He thought, I wonder what would happen if I kissed her, and wished he could ask, but he had run out of badges.

Jan Mark: "I do not wear badges myself, but I collect them for my son, who does not wear them either – he just likes having *them, and it was at a book fair, of which institution this story features a very unfair*

131

description, that I first saw a badge-making machine in action. Incidentally, it's not true that all writers look like teachers, although a number have been teachers, and some still are. I never wrote any books while I was teaching. I was too tired."

Heinemann
New Windmills

Founding Editors: Anne and Ian Serraillier

Chinua Achebe Things Fall Apart
Vivien Alcock The Cuckoo Sister; The Monster Garden;
The Trial of Anna Cotman; A Kind of Thief; Ghostly Companions
Margaret Atwood The Handmaid's Tale
Jane Austen Pride and Prejudice
J G Ballard Empire of the Sun
Nina Bawden The Witch's Daughter; A Handful of Thieves; Carrie's
War; The Robbers; Devil by the Sea; Kept in the Dark; The Finding;
Keeping Henry; Humbug; The Outside Child
Valerie Bierman No More School
Melvin Burgess An Angel for May
Ray Bradbury The Golden Apples of the Sun; The Illustrated Man
Betsy Byars The Midnight Fox; Goodbye, Chicken Little; The
Pinballs; The Not-Just-Anybody Family; The Eighteenth Emergency
Victor Canning The Runaways; Flight of the Grey Goose
Ann Coburn Welcome to the Real World
Hannah Cole Bring in the Spring
Jane Leslie Conly Racso and the Rats of NIMH
Robert Cormier We All Fall Down; Tunes for Bears to Dance to
Roald Dahl Danny, The Champion of the World; The Wonderful
Story of Henry Sugar; George's Marvellous Medicine; The BFG;
The Witches; Boy; Going Solo; Matilda
Anita Desai The Village by the Sea
Charles Dickens A Christmas Carol; Great Expectations;
Hard Times; Oliver Twist; A Charles Dickens Selection
Peter Dickinson Merlin Dreams
Berlie Doherty Granny was a Buffer Girl; Street Child
Roddy Doyle Paddy Clarke Ha Ha Ha
Gerald Durrell My Family and Other Animals
Anne Fine The Granny Project
Anne Frank The Diary of Anne Frank
Leon Garfield Six Apprentices; Six Shakespeare Stories;
Six More Shakespeare Stories
Jamila Gavin The Wheel of Surya
Adele Geras Snapshots of Paradise

Alan Gibbons Chicken
Graham Greene The Third Man and The Fallen Idol; Brighton Rock
Thomas Hardy The Withered Arm and Other Wessex Tales
L P Hartley The Go-Between
Ernest Hemmingway The Old Man and the Sea; A Farewell to Arms
Nigel Hinton Getting Free; Buddy; Buddy's Song
Anne Holm I Am David
Janni Howker Badger on the Barge; Isaac Campion; Martin Farrell
Jennifer Johnston Shadows on Our Skin
Toeckey Jones Go Well, Stay Well
Geraldine Kaye Comfort Herself; A Breath of Fresh Air
Clive King Me and My Million
Dick King-Smith The Sheep-Pig
Daniel Keyes Flowers for Algernon
Elizabeth Laird Red Sky in the Morning; Kiss the Dust
D H Lawrence The Fox and The Virgin and the Gypsy;
Selected Tales
Harper Lee To Kill a Mockingbird
Ursula Le Guin A Wizard of Earthsea
Julius Lester Basketball Game
C Day Lewis The Otterbury Incident
David Line Run for Your Life
Joan Lingard Across the Barricades; Into Exile; The Clearance;
The File on Fraulein Berg
Robin Lister The Odyssey
Penelope Lively The Ghost of Thomas Kempe
Jack London The Call of the Wild; White Fang
Bernard Mac Laverty Cal; The Best of Bernard Mac Laverty
Margaret Mahy The Haunting
Jan Mark Do You Read Me? (Eight Short Stories)
James Vance Marshall Walkabout
W Somerset Maughan The Kite and Other Stories
Ian McEwan The Daydreamer; A Child in Time
Pat Moon The Spying Game
Michael Morpurgo Waiting for Anya; My Friend Walter;
The War of Jenkins' Ear
Bill Naughton The Goalkeeper's Revenge
New Windmill A Charles Dickens Selection
New Windmill Book of Classic Short Stories
New Windmill Book of Nineteenth Century Short Stories

How many have you read?